"You're going to have to trust me, Katie."

Alec's fingers tightened briefly before falling away and she missed the connection immediately. She placed a hand on his chest and when she did, both of them went instantly still. Tension radiated from his body. His breathing became shallower. She met his gaze and saw the desire there. Her pulse kicked a little harder and her throat tightened. When she'd reached out for him, she'd intended to ask him to hold her. She'd thought the only thing she wanted from him was to feel safe. But looking into his eyes, she felt anything but that.

Uncertain, Katie dropped her gaze to his throat. Smooth skin. The scent of his cologne reaching her. The open collar of his shirt left a triangle of skin exposed. What would his chest be like? What would it feel like to lay her hand over his heart without a shirt in the way? To feel smooth male flesh beneath her palm instead of starched cotton? Letting her hand drop, she backed away. It took her another second to look at him again.

"I trust you, Alec," she whispered, but was surprised by just how unsteady her voice was when she said it.

TARGETED
LORI L. HARRIS

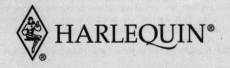

TORONTO • NEW YORK • LONDON
AMSTERDAM • PARIS • SYDNEY • HAMBURG
STOCKHOLM • ATHENS • TOKYO • MILAN • MADRID
PRAGUE • WARSAW • BUDAPEST • AUCKLAND

I need to thank fellow critique partners Terri Backhus, Ann Bair and Kathleen Pynn for their unending generosity. And fellow suspense author Kathy Holzapfel for her devious mind, quick wit and friendship. Without these four, writing wouldn't be nearly the adventure that it is.

And as always, to my very own hero, Bobby Harris.

ISBN 0-373-22901-1

TARGETED

Copyright © 2006 by Lori L. Harris

www.eHarlequin.com

Printed in U.S.A.

ABOUT THE AUTHOR

Lori Harris has always enjoyed competition. She grew up in southern Ohio, showing Arabian horses and Great Danes. Later she joined a shooting league where she competed head-to-head with police officers—and would be competing today if she hadn't discovered how much fun and challenging it was to write. Romantic suspense seemed a natural fit. What could be more exciting than writing about life-and-death struggles that include sexy, strong men?

When not in front of a computer, Lori enjoys remodeling her home, gardening and boating. Lori lives in Orlando, Florida, with her very own hero.

Books by Lori L. Harris

HARLEQUIN INTRIGUE
830—SOMEONE SAFE
901—TARGETED

Dear Reader,

When I was thinking about the setting for *Targeted*, the first in a pair of stories about THE BLADE BROTHERS OF COUGAR COUNTY, I knew immediately that it would be Florida. From the very first moment I set foot in the state more than twenty years ago, she has always held a certain mystery for me. On the surface, she's sunny beaches and sparkling salt water, modern cities with mass transit and sophisticated nightlife. But that's just the garb she wears, not who she really is.

You have to get off the beaten track to discover Florida's true beauty—the dark, tea-colored waters of her mangrove swamps, the large expanses of her real estate owned more by the alligators and mosquitoes that inhabit them than the investors who hold title to them. Wide open prairies where cattle graze in knee-high grasses and cowboys still ride out to check on them. And the small towns where a hitching post still stands out front—a reminder that no matter how much we seem to move beyond our pasts, we never fully leave them behind.

Alec Blade and Katie Carroll, the hero and heroine of *Targeted,* are both attempting to do just that, though, when they move to Deep Water, Florida. They believe it's possible to file away the unresolved events of their violent pasts. But they learn just how mistaken they are when one of those faceless monsters reappears. Suddenly it isn't a matter of outrunning the past. Now they have to survive long enough to have a future.

Hang on as Alec and Katie fight for their lives—and somewhere along the way, they'll discover a passion neither of them has ever experienced.

Warmly,

Lori Harris

Chapter One

As soon as Alec Blade stepped inside Frankie's Gun and Range, the dull thuds of live rounds slamming into plate steel at a velocity of more than eight hundred feet per second resounded.

The rottweiler that had been dozing at the end of the long display counter climbed to his feet even before the range marshal looked up. The man was somewhere deep in his sixties, on the lean side, wearing a bowling shirt with *Frankie* embroidered on the chest. His smile was welcoming enough. Until he spotted the telltale bulge of a weapon beneath Alec's jacket.

He reached for something beneath the desk. "I need to see a badge or a concealed weapon permit."

"Sure." Alec handed over the newly acquired State of Florida permit, and while it was being inspected, glanced at the rottweiler that now sat two feet away with pricked ears and watchful eyes.

"Beautiful dog. Does he have a name?" Alec asked.

"Teddy Bear."

Alec guessed the dog's weight to be in the one-fifty range, most of it in the massive head and jaws, the thick, muscled neck. "Interesting choice of a name. Sort of like calling a Great Dane, Tiny."

"My wife named him as a pup. It fit back then. Teddy, give the man a smile."

The dog's heavy dewlaps drew back to reveal a very impressive set of teeth. It was like looking into the eyes of a sociopath. The mouth said one thing; the eyes said something far more deadly. Intent on keeping both hands, Alec left them resting on the display case.

Satisfied, Frankie passed back the permit. "Any relation to our new police chief?"

Sensing his services weren't needed, the rottweiler wandered back to a spot at the end of the counter and plopped down.

Alec returned his wallet to his back pocket before answering. "Brother. I was told he was shooting here."

The man checked the log book on the counter. "In the sixth bay. I got a spot next to him open."

"No, thanks. Is he alone in there?"

"No. Got a lesson going in bay three, but it should be over in a few minutes." Frankie grabbed a form from the pile next to the cash register. "Even if you're not shooting, you'll need to sign the waiver."

He pointed to the signature line beneath several paragraphs of small print. His blue-tinged nail bed suggested the beginning stages of lead poisoning, a fairly common problem for people who owned and ran indoor ranges.

"You can read it if you want, but it just says you won't hold it against me if they cart you out of here on a gurney. Or in a body bag."

"Sounds reasonable." Alec took the pen.

"And you'll need eyes and ears." Frankie retrieved

shooting glasses and earmuffs from a box on the floor behind him and laid them on the counter.

After putting on both, Alec opened the heavy door separating the store from the range, and the noise escalated. Since leaving the FBI nearly a year ago, he hadn't had a reason to visit an indoor facility, but the scent of cordite was still familiar, as was the strong percussion of a forty-five caliber round ripping through paper before flattening against the back wall.

The first bays were empty, the lights off, and the target hanger waiting for paper. The third contained a well-dressed business-type woman working with an instructor. From the look of it, it wasn't the first lesson for the good-looking, twentysomething blonde.

His brother was at the end and in the process of emptying his weapon in rapid fire. When the chamber locked open, Jack ejected the empty magazine from the Colt and, after lowering the gun to the weapon rest, reloaded one of the three magazines in front of him. The blue-gray haze of spent gunpowder lingered in the dimly lit space.

He wasn't as tall as Alec, only six foot to Alec's six-two, and there was little in facial features or coloring to suggest shared DNA. Jack was blond, blue-eyed to Alec's darker coloring.

There was more than six years between them, enough so that they hadn't been close growing up. Alec's fault, of course, since he was the older sibling. Even the death of their parents four years ago hadn't narrowed the gap. He regretted the distance, as he regretted so many things these days. Part of the reason he'd relocated to Cougar County was to mend their relationship. That, and he'd had nowhere else to go after he'd buried his wife.

Jack looked up and saw Alec. "Been there long?"

"Just got here."

Jack thumbed the last round into the magazine, and then pressed the button to recall the target.

"Planning to shoot a few?"

"No. I went by the office, and your dispatcher said you usually stopped by here on Wednesday nights."

"Wanda did?" Jack loaded the second magazine. "Suppose I'll have to change my schedule, then."

"Why?"

"Because I like some degree of privacy." Jack replaced the paper target, sent it out to the fifteen-yard mark. "And I'm sure you're very aware by now that, in a town the size of Deep Water, it's hard to come by."

Soon after he'd relocated to Deep Water, with its brick streets and quaint shops, Alec had learned that Southern towns were not the place to go if you wanted privacy. At one time Deep Water had been Cougar County's seat, a destination for wealthy Northerners looking for a place to winter. Today it was a town that had been forced to find ways to reinvent itself after an interstate highway had suddenly put it off the beaten path.

Alec took the target his brother passed to him. "Not bad." There was a nice grouping in the chest region. He pointed to the head shots. "You're pushing these."

"You think you can do better?"

Raising his hands in a gesture of surrender, Alec took a step back. Even if he'd had the time, he wasn't about to get into a pissing contest with his brother. That was part of the problem in their relationship. Too much of the wrong kind of competitiveness in recent years.

"Didn't think so." Jack closed up the box of ammo he'd been loading from and placed it in the bag at his feet before jumping to the question of why Alec was there. "Did the postcard come?"

Alec shoved his hands into his pockets. "No." It wasn't a subject that he wanted to pursue.

Once a month, for the past eleven months, starting the day after the murder of Jill Blade, a postcard had arrived from the UNSUB—the unknown subject—with one word typed on it: REMEMBER. The postcard was always the cheap variety that could be purchased almost anywhere, but the typewriter that had been used and the postmark changed each time.

Jack seemed to gauge Alec's reaction to this change in pattern.

"Do you think the fact you didn't get one means something?" Jack asked.

"Sure. The post office screwed up. The UNSUB's in prison. Or he's dead. Or he lost track of time."

"Or maybe he's grown tired of the game," Jack said quietly.

Alec chose to ignore the observation. Perhaps because he couldn't bear to contemplate the possibility. Though it was painful to get them, if the cards stopped coming, what then? With viable leads drying up, the cards were the only tie he had with Jill's killer. And perhaps his only hope of seeing him behind bars.

And capturing his wife's killer, seeing him brought to justice, was the reason he'd left the Bureau and the reason he got up most mornings.

Jack placed a second pistol case on the shooting bench. A SIG-Sauer. Even as a kid, Jack had collected toys.

"So why were you looking for me?"

The door between the range and the store opened briefly as the woman and instructor left.

"I got a phone call about an hour ago," Alec said. "I'm heading out of town."

"A consulting job?"

After leaving the Bureau, he'd opened a company that dealt with post 9/11 security. He'd expected to generate enough business to pay the bills while he hunted Jill's killer, but because of his expertise and his security clearance, he'd had more business than he could handle alone.

"No. Not a consulting job. The detective on Jill's case is interviewing a suspect they're holding in connection with a rape and he wants me to sit in tomorrow morning."

Jack frowned. "Does he look good for Jill's murder?"

"No. But he claims to have information. Probably just looking to cut a deal." Alec suspected it was another dead end, but he couldn't afford to ignore a lead.

Jack wiped his hands on a towel. "So you just came by to tell me you were leaving town?"

"Yeah." Alec had never bothered in the past, which made it awkward as hell now. He'd spent so much of his life coming and going, never filling in anyone—including his wife—on his actions.

Early in their marriage, when Jill had pressed him to talk about his work, he'd made the mistake of giving in to her demands and telling her too much about a case. For several weeks afterward, though she'd tried to pretend it hadn't changed things between them, he knew it had. She'd seemed almost reluctant to let him touch her. And he'd desperately needed that connection to keep him human.

After that, he'd been more careful with what he shared. He'd talk about investigations and cases and court trials, but never about the atrocities, nor about decayed bodies, nor about mutilated women or murdered children.

Jack slid a magazine into the SIG-Sauer, chambered the

first round. He shifted his right foot forward and brought the weapon up into the Weaver position, his index finger resting lightly alongside the trigger guard.

"Are you sure I can't talk you into a little head-to-head brotherly competition? I win, I get the details of your date tonight. Nothing personal. Just whether you have a good time. Whether she's a good conversationalist."

Alec felt irritation kick in. He knew he shouldn't be annoyed with Jack. But these days he found himself feeling a lot of things, including isolation, that he didn't want to. Perhaps that was why he'd impulsively asked Katie Carroll out.

"How did you find out about that?"

"I heard it from one of the deputies who heard it from one of Katie's coworkers."

Katie waited tables at Alligator Café where he had breakfast most mornings. She had a quick smile, but he'd recently learned that she wasn't quite the open book that she wanted people to believe she was. In addition to waiting tables, she was a well-known Miami artist.

Jack lowered his weapon. "Of course, with the way you've been watching her all these weeks, it doesn't really come as a surprise."

"It isn't really a date," Alec said.

Jack grinned. "If you ask a woman out and it involves food, it's a date."

"Doesn't matter what you call it because my flight leaves at nine thirty tonight, so I have to cancel."

The smile fading, Jack placed the gun on the rest again. "A morning flight wouldn't have done just as well? Hell, even one a few hours later tonight?"

"It's just pizza and conversation. She's new in town. I'm new in town. No big deal." Alec wondered why he felt compelled to tell his brother anything. Next time he'd just leave a message on his voice mail.

"Wrong. It's the first time you've made any attempt to join the living." Jack's mouth flattened. "I was happy for you. You were actually going to share the twentieth of the month with a live woman instead of a dead one."

Controlling his irritation this time wasn't nearly as easy, but Alec managed.

When he remained silent, Jack's expression turned more troubled. "I'm sorry if that sounds cruel or cold. I don't mean it that way. You know how I felt about Jill. But the interview's not until tomorrow. Change your flight. Go out with Katie tonight. Get on with your life."

Alec took a deep breath and let it out slowly. "Let's not do this, okay?"

Turning away, he headed for the door, feeling dissatisfied. Not just with his brother and their relationship, but with everything. He'd made a career out of hunting down the worst kind of men. Human predators that killed for the sheer sport of it. But when it came to tracking down his own wife's killer, he couldn't get the job done. He'd failed Jill while she was alive. And he was failing her now.

"Jill loved you, Alec. She'd want you to move on."

Alec paused and looked back. "Let's not pretend we have any inkling what the other one needs. Maybe if you had been where I've been…"

"You've forgotten where I've been, haven't you?" Jack immediately went back to firing his weapon. As if Alec was already gone.

Jack had spent five years undercover in Atlanta. A hard life where you were cut off from everything and everyone. It was their single shared characteristic. Their inability to achieve any kind of real intimacy with another human being. Alec recognized it in himself, but he suspected his brother was still in denial.

Bottom line, though, they were brothers. And they were all the family either one of them had. As adults, they should be able to find some middle ground.

Instead of leaving, Alec waited until Jack had emptied the gun. "I'll call you when I get back. Maybe we can get a beer."

Jack hesitated as if he debated saying more, but then settled for a simple, "Sure. A beer." Jack tucked his weapon into his shoulder holster. "Since you're not interested in Katie, I think I'll give her a call while you're gone. She's a good-looking woman. And she has the air of mystery about her that I find appealing."

Alec knew what Jack was trying to do. He gave his brother a wry grin that said it wasn't going to work. "Jealousy is a pointless emotion based on insecurities."

Jack didn't return the grin. "Yes. But at least it is an emotion."

KATIE CARROLL opened her front door just after six forty-five. She did her nightly battle with the door lock—a task made that much more difficult because she was carrying dry cleaning on one arm and a bag of groceries on the other. Of course, it didn't help that she was in a hurry and had less than thirty minutes to wash and dry her hair and straighten the place before her date arrived.

Even though Alec Blade had been drawing her into more and more conversations over the past few weeks, she'd still been surprised this morning when he'd asked her out.

When she'd finally wrestled the key free, she turned and clicked on the porch and foyer lights, and then closed the door behind her.

But as soon as she turned the dead bolt, she felt her pulse accelerate, felt the sharp tingling sensation climb her spine. *Please, not again.* It had been weeks since she'd had an anxiety attack. Long enough that she'd thought she was over them.

The familiar tightness in her chest intensified, until it felt as if she was trapped inside a burning room, and the searing, thick air had been robbed of oxygen. Sweat trailed down her rib cage. She held the plastic dry-cleaning bag and grocery sack in front of her like armor.

Closing her eyes, she fell back on the mantra the psychologist had helped her create at her last appointment. "I am safe." She paused, focusing on what she'd just said before moving on to the next affirmation. "Nothing's going to happen to me." She concentrated on drawing air into her lungs, too, this time. "Because I won't allow it to happen. Because I am in control."

Logically, Katie recognized that she had nothing to fear. That there was no one out to get her. But panic attacks weren't based in logic.

"I am safe. Nothing's going to happen to me," she repeated until slowly, her breathing returned to normal, and she managed to release her hold on the sack. It took nearly another minute before she could make herself move from in front of the door.

As she did, she glanced into the living room and immediately froze. The front drapes were drawn. Had she left this morning without opening them? Had the fact that they were closed registered subconsciously? Was that all it had taken to set off the attack?

Then she spotted the envelope propped on the mantel. Her landlord. She should have known he'd show up when she wasn't around. He'd done the same with the bad plug in the bathroom. He'd come while she was at work. When she'd come home that night, she'd found his pliers on her unmade bed.

The next day she'd purchased and installed chains on all the doors. She couldn't keep him out when she wasn't here, but she damn well wasn't going to have to worry about him walking in on her.

She ripped the envelope down and removed the note inside.

YOUR LEASE REQUIRES YOU TO GET WRITTEN APPROVAL BEFORE MAKING ANY CHANGES TO THE PROPERTY!!

KITCHEN LEAK WILL REQUIRE A FEW PARTS. BE BACK NEXT WEEK. PLEASE KEEP DRAPES DRAWN DURING DAY AND THERMOSTAT OFF UNLESS YOU'RE HOME.
ELECTRICITY IS EXPENSIVE!

Irritated, she tossed it down. Did he really consider the door chains a change to the property? That was one thing she wouldn't miss when she moved. Her landlord. He really creeped her out at times.

When she turned on the lamp at the end of the sofa, she noticed just how dusty the table was. After using her hand to clear the worst of it, she examined the other pieces of furniture. Two equally hideous reproduction side chairs from different Louis eras flanked the drab olive sofa, one end of which had become the depository for her collection of art catalogues.

She hadn't had anyone over since she'd moved in, so hadn't given much thought to how ugly the room was.

Either she could straighten up the room, or she could take a quick shower. Suspecting her date would be more impressed with a female who didn't smell like a diner—grease and raw eggs—she headed for the kitchen.

Katie jumped when the kitchen wall phone rang as she walked past. Considering how few people had her number, it would have to be her parents. If she answered it, there would be no shower. With each unanswered ring, her guilt-index crept higher, until finally she hung the dry cleaning on a hook just inside the door and reached for the phone. Just as the ringing stopped.

Relief rolled over her. She'd tried, right? And she could just call her folks later. With the time difference, they'd still be up when she got home.

Enough light followed her from the living room into the kitchen that she didn't bother to turn on the overhead light in the small room. The curtains for the window over the sink were in the washing machine, and she didn't like the idea that anyone could stand outside and watch her movements.

After quickly unloading groceries onto the green-tiled counter, she grabbed a plate for the cheese and crackers. The soft tap of water against the sink bottom forced her to cross to the kitchen sink. Darn drip. If anything, it was worse.

She set the wine bottle on the counter and gave the faucet handle a hard turn. Leave it to her landlord to be so darned eager to conserve electricity while wasting water.

Behind her, the floorboard creaked. The old flooring under her feet gave slightly. Her lungs tightened as with sudden clarity, she realized she wasn't alone. Worse, that she hadn't been alone from the moment she'd walked in tonight.

Don't panic. Think. The last thing she needed was to be

frozen with terror. She'd taken a self-defense course. She knew what to do. Flee if possible. If that wasn't an option…

"Lousy faucet," she said softly, pretending to try it again. What did the intruder want? Not money. If he'd wanted cash, he'd have already taken it from her jewelry box. He wouldn't be standing behind her now.

The hairs at the back of her neck stood out, and her back muscles, even her abdominals, clenched in fear.

From the corner of her eye, she glanced at the back door. Too far. She'd never make it. She looked out the window over the sink. Toward her closest neighbor's house. The light in their side yard was barely visible through the trees. They wouldn't hear or see anything.

And then she saw the silhouette in the glass. A large man. Moving toward her.

Still twisting the faucet handle with her right hand, Katie reached for the drawer to the left of the sink, the one where she kept knives. She slid it open and stuck her hand inside. She could feel the cool, solid hardness of the bone handle. She could do this. She had to do this. She had to protect herself.

An arm suddenly smashed across her ribs as a second locked around her throat. She was hauled backward. The drawer came with her, but the edge of the cabinet caught the knife and ripped it from her fingers.

Knives and ladles and spatulas clattered across the oak floor like pickup sticks in a deadly game. At the last moment, she grabbed for the wine bottle but only managed to knock it over. As it hit the floor, it exploded. A chunk of flying glass clipped her shin and warm wine splattered her legs.

Katie brought her heel down hard, but she was wearing soft soles. Her attacker shifted just enough to deflect the blow. Utensils clanked. Kicking them aside, the man lifted her off the ground, his muscular arm driving the air from her lungs. He swung her toward the hall doorway. Pain exploded as her kneecap slammed into the oak jamb. The blow dislodged the wall phone's handset and it crashed toward the floor, and then leaped upward like a bungee jumper.

Glass ground beneath his boots, chewing the wood floor.

"No!" Katie latched on to the door trim.

Her fingernails bent backward, separating from their beds. She lost her hold. She jammed her elbow into his ribs. He barely flinched. She grabbed his ear, the only vulnerable area she could reach, and dug in her nails.

Grunting, the man slammed her headfirst against the hall wall and pinned her there. With her head turned to the side and canted upward at an angle, movement was impossible. His heavy body continued to press in on her from behind. And still she hung on to his ear, knowing that if she let go, he'd kill her.

It was then she smelled the candle wax. Shifting her gaze toward her barely opened bedroom door, she saw the candlelight playing across the scuffed hall floor.

How long had this man been here—in her house—preparing for what he was going to do to her? The horror of what was about to happen forced the last of the air from her lungs.

He leaned in harder. She felt the vertebrae of her neck strain.

She should have answered the phone, talked to her parents. Oh, God, she wanted to hear their voices one last time.

And then, when she was completely immobile, completely powerless, she heard his voice for the first time.

"Did you really think I'd let you live, Katydid?"

Chapter Two

Thirty-five minutes after leaving the shooting range and his brother, Alec parked in front of Katie's bungalow. He'd tried phoning to cancel their date. But when he'd gotten her voice mail, he'd resigned himself to stopping by with a pizza.

His right hand propped on the steering wheel, he glanced at the cut flowers resting on the carry-out pizza box. He'd picked up the bouquet at the supermarket. The female clerk had thought him cheap for buying the very last of the mixed bunches. The center of some of the flowers had already turned brown. But his only other choice had been the old standby of red roses, and he couldn't make himself pick them up.

"Say it with flowers."

Grabbing the pizza and the bouquet, he climbed out of the SUV. Five minutes tops. He'd hand her the pizza and the flowers, wish her a good night and a good life.

The Azalea Park neighborhood, which had been built in the second decade of the last century, was one of those up-and-coming areas. Most of the people took care of their properties, but there were a few holdouts who seemed content with sparse lawns, overgrown shrubs and peeling paint.

Surrounded by an out-of-control hedge, the entry courtyard of Katie's Spanish bungalow was dark. After knocking, he waited. When she didn't answer, he checked his watch. Seven ten. He was early. Maybe she was running late getting home or was in the shower.

Alec changed the flowers to his other hand, and, lightly popping the cellophane-encased bouquet against his pant leg, debated just leaving a note.

A loud crash came from inside. Then breaking glass.

What in the hell was going on? He tried the door. "Katie?"

A woman screamed.

Tossing down flowers and pizza, Alec pulled the Glock from his shoulder holster. With a solid kick, he forced the dead bolt through the frame. The door slammed into the wall behind, the glass in the top half shattering upon impact.

Katie's and her attacker's shadows briefly filled the hallway.

Bursting low and fast through the open door, he chose the unlit room to the right. Reaching it, he pressed himself hard against the wall, trying to leave the suspect with as little of a target as possible.

Alec inched forward. A large chunk of plaster exploded several inches from his face. A second round immediately hit in nearly the same spot. A controlled double tap. This wasn't some street thug. And it sure as hell wasn't a Saturday night special.

Alec knew he was moving too fast, recklessly. He needed to slow down. He needed to get his adrenaline under control.

"FBI," he yelled, but made no move to advance.

Nothing. No indication of movement anywhere in the house. Alec tried not to think about what that might mean. That Katie was already dead. Or seriously injured.

He wasn't even sure what he was dealing with here—a

burglary attempt that had hit the skids or attempted rape. Jesus. He had hoped never to face another situation like this.

"Put down your weapon," Alec ordered.

No response again. He scanned what appeared to be the dining room for another entrance. Finding none, he realized he'd made a poor choice. With the only way in or out either this door or the front window, he was pinned down. Of course, at the time, a dark room had seemed a better choice than a well-lit one.

Alec's heart hammered. With no other choice, he slid around the door frame and into the entry foyer again, into the light spilling from the living room. The house was cold and silent. A clock ticked somewhere, or maybe it was some type of drip. He'd once entered the bathroom of a murder victim, expecting to turn off a faucet's slow drip only to discover the sound had nothing to do with plumbing.

He could hear movement now and advanced toward it. The wood floor creaked with the slightest of weight shift, making silent progress impossible. And having never been in this house, he didn't know the layout, but assumed the hall led to bedrooms and at least one bathroom. There would also be a kitchen, which he would have expected to connect with the dining room, so there was no telling where it fell in the floor plan. But all these old houses had a second door, usually off the kitchen. Was the suspect trying to reach it?

Sensing he was about to step into the path of a bullet, Alec ran his left hand over his chest—the habit, a hangover from his Bureau days, was meant to assure him that his soft body armor was in place. Of course, he was a civilian now, and civilians had no need for the protective powers of Kevlar. Not unless they were going into a dark house, facing a shooter who obviously knew how to handle his weapon.

A soft whimper that was quickly squashed. Leading with his own weapon, Alec stepped from the foyer into the narrow hall leading toward the back of the house. The front door was open behind him, and the way the night air poured into the small foyer and down the hall suggested that there was another open door or window ahead of him somewhere.

The darkness was more complete here, the only light coming from beneath the closed door at the end of the hall. Alec ignored the room as a possibility, concentrated on the other three doors. In his head, he heard Monty asking which door it would be.

He held his position again, listening. With the elapsed time, it became more likely that the suspect intended to shoot it out.

A sharp clatter. Alec moved forward in a controlled rush. By the time he reached the door into the kitchen, fresh air poured through the opened back door, as did the glow from the side yard light. He caught a glimpse of the suspect fleeing down the steps. As much as he wanted to pursue the man, he needed to determine Katie's where-abouts and condition, so he turned and faced the room.

"Katie?"

Even with the light penetrating only three or four feet inside, he could see the mess on the floor. The glittering shards of glass, the sheen of a dark liquid, the shine of stainless implements. The skeletons of overturned dinette chairs.

What he didn't see, what he might not have seen at all if she hadn't made a sound somewhere between a gasp and a sob, was Katie slumped against the old refrigerator.

She was drawn up in a near-fetal position. He kneeled down, but didn't touch her; he was afraid that even that small contact might send her over the edge.

"Katie?" She lifted her chin slightly as if she looked at him, but he couldn't be certain. "Katie, I need you to answer me. Are you hurt?"

She shook her head.

"I need to go after the man who did this to you. Do you understand?" He thought she nodded. "Call 9-1-1."

He'd taken only a single step when she launched herself after him, her hands grabbing at his legs, her movements sending kitchen utensils clanging. "No. He'll come back. He'll kill me."

Alec kneeled next to her again. "Easy. I won't be gone long." He picked up a knife and pressed it into her hands. "Hold on to this."

Taking it, she scooted backward until she was once more plastered to the appliance.

Alec checked the side yard where legustroms and large oleanders blocked the house next door. He'd lost too much time in the kitchen. The suspect could be anywhere by now.

Frustration building, Alec circled to the front of the house to scan the street. Everything was quiet.

He reentered through the back door. He'd no sooner flipped on the overhead light, than Katie scrambled up from her position on the floor beneath the phone and turned it off. "No lights. He'll see us."

In the strobe of illumination, Alec had seen the mess, not just on the floor, but also throughout the room. The struggle had been both drawn out and vicious. The only surprise was, for whatever reason, Katie was still alive. She had somehow survived.

"Take it easy, Katie."

After sliding his weapon into the shoulder holster, he squatted cautiously next to her. "Give me the knife." She let him take it from her, and he placed it beyond her reach. When he touched her on the shoulder, she jerked and lifted her left hand in a defensive motion, as if to ward off any further attempts at contact.

Ignoring the broken glass, he carefully sat down in front of her.

"Katie, did you dial 9-1-1?"

She nodded. Using one finger, he caught her chin and urged it higher. Her face was wet. She was crying, he realized. He couldn't tell much about her eyes in the dark, but when she trembled, he realized he didn't need to see dilated pupils to know she was in shock. She was frightened beyond belief.

"Did you—" He had intended to ask her about the attack, but quickly stopped himself. Habits were hard to shake. Especially in stressful situations. He'd spent too many years in charge, accustomed to asking the questions. But it was no longer his job. And there was no reason to put her through it twice.

He was unprepared when she suddenly buried her face against his chest. He raised his arms, uncertain. After a brief hesitation, he wrapped them around her.

For the first time in eleven months, Alec held a woman. And sitting there in the darkened kitchen, he couldn't help but think how different tonight would have been if he'd left that voice mail. If he hadn't decided he owed her an explanation in person.

And how one moment in a man's life, a woman's life, could define everything that followed.

OH GOD, oh God, oh God.

Katie's fist twisted tighter into Alec's shirt as she burrowed her face into his shoulder. The sirens were just outside now. How long had she—had they—been sitting on the floor? Probably no more than six or seven minutes, but it seemed far longer.

Her body moved in a rocking motion, but she seemed powerless to stop it, or even to alter the timing of it. She wasn't even sure if the motion was of her doing or of the man's who held her. But the rhythm of his heart had become a calming metronome.

If she could just concentrate on the heavy, steady beat. If she could just stay here. In the dark. In these strong arms. She would be okay.

"Police," a man's voice called from the foyer.

She felt Alec moving away from her, physically and emotionally. Her fingers squeezed the material of his sleeve. If she let him go, she didn't know what would happen.

"In here," Alec called. "In the kitchen."

Heavy footsteps moved down the hall. Flashlight beams stabbed and probed until they found them. The light switch, a relic from the twenties, made a sharp click.

Three men, Police Chief Jack Blade and two young deputies whose names she didn't know, stood in the doorway.

Squinting against the sudden glare, she pushed herself off Alec's lap and onto the floor, wincing as broken glass bit into her palm. She kept her eyes averted, was afraid that, if she looked at any of the men who now stared at her, she'd lose the little bit of self-control that she'd managed to regain over the past few minutes.

"Katie?"

Looking up, she realized Alec was on his feet now, and was offering her a hand up. His face was grim. For the first time she registered the shoulder holster and the gun. She'd never seen him with a weapon of any sort, so she was put off by it. Which was really ridiculous, considering what had happened tonight. When his warm fingers closed over her frigid ones, she realized that even that small contact made her feel safer.

Once she was standing, he kept a hand locked around her arm as if he didn't trust her to stay on her feet. And maybe he was right to, because she felt woozy.

"You out riding patrols tonight?" Alec asked his brother.

"No. Just in the area when the call came in." Chief Blade looked at Katie. "Do you want a ride to the hospital?"

"No. I'm fine." She touched the side of her face, testing the soreness. Well, maybe not fine, but the hospital was still out. She hated anything to do with them.

The chief nudged the closest officer—a young kid who looked as if he should still be in high school. "Take the front door. I don't want anyone coming in until Martinez is done processing the scene." His glance skipped to the second officer. "Fitz, get some more manpower over here to check the neighborhood. I want everyone who's available." As the man walked away, he added, "And get the pizza box and flowers off the front porch. Throw them both on my floorboard."

The police chief swung his attention back to his brother. "I'm assuming you brought both?"

Alec ignored his brother's question. "I'm not sure how he got in, but he went out through that door." He nodded toward the still open back one. "I went after him, so you'll find my shoeprints out there, too."

The police chief frowned. "Did you check the other rooms?"

"No. I figured you'd be showing up soon enough. That the fewer people walking through the house, possibly disturbing evidence, the better. You'll find a couple of bullets meant for me near the dining room entrance and my fingerprints from the front door on through to the kitchen."

"Martinez will need comparison prints."

"Whenever he wants them." Alec lifted Katie's right hand. "He'll probably want to check out her fingernails just in case some of that blood belongs to the suspect." He let her hand go. She wished he hadn't.

Chief Blade gave a sharp nod. "Helpful, as always, Alec." There was an edge to his voice that Katie didn't understand. But then she didn't know him. Maybe it was the situation. Situation? Now there was a euphemism for what had happened to her.

Once she was seated on the sofa, Alec brought her a glass of water. Glancing down, she caught sight of her black and blue left knee and felt the first hard throb of pain.

It was as if her body was a computer that had been shut down, but now booted up, each program reporting its status at regular intervals. Now the face. Now the neck. And now the knee. She suspected the worst was yet to come.

And not just physically. There would be questions. Ones that she would find difficult to answer.

Jack pulled up a chair opposite while Alec chose to stand at the foyer door. As irrational as it sounded, she would have liked to have Alec sitting next to her while his brother asked his questions, but didn't know how to make the request without appearing needy.

Who was she trying to kid? She was needy. But she could handle her own neediness.

The police chief waited until she swung her gaze back to him. Jack Blade was younger than Alec by a few years, and with his blond hair, he looked more like a lifeguard than a lawman. She had heard rumors that he'd worked undercover in a big city before he'd come to Deep Water. But

Deep Water's rumor mill was wrong more often than right. She only had to look at what they said about her to know that.

"Katie, I need you to start at the beginning and tell me everything you can remember."

She nodded, but swallowed roughly. Her neck and throat hurt from the choke hold.

"Any possibility that you know your attacker? Have you ever seen him before?"

She shook her head. "No. At least I don't think so."

"When you came home, was he already in the house?"

"Yes. But I don't know where. Maybe in my bedroom. Or in the hall closet." She ducked her head. Not meeting his eyes made it easier to talk about. "He…he came up behind me while I was at the kitchen sink and….and—" She couldn't seem to go on. When the police chief reached out to touch her in a comforting gesture, she moved her hand just beyond his reach.

He acted as if he hadn't noticed the movement, but she knew he had. "Take your time. There's no hurry."

She nodded her understanding. Instead of easier, she was finding it more difficult to control her emotions. Maybe it was due to the adrenaline. But she didn't like the way she was right now. She didn't want to be this person.

"He wanted…" He wanted to kill her. She still couldn't believe it, but it had to be true. There was no other explanation. "I got away. Made it to the back door. But he'd taken the key."

After taking a small sip of water, just enough to moisten her tongue, she managed to continue. "I used a chair to break the glass. He…he got to me before…I could get out. He dragged me into the hall."

She turned to Alec. "That's when you showed up."

"Any chance you might recognize him if you saw him again?" the police chief asked.

"Maybe." She heard the doubt in her own voice, and realized that she was shaking her head slowly. "I'm not sure, it…was dark. He didn't really allow me to see his face."

"I understand. Was he tall? Big?"

"Both," she said, thinking about the hard mass of his body.

Alec straightened in the doorway, but kept his arms folded. "He was six-one or two, probably went two-twenty or more."

"You got a look at him?" Chief Blade asked his brother.

"Not a very long one, and, as Katie said, it was dark."

Chief Blade turned his attention back to her. "Caucasian?"

She nodded. "I think so."

"But you're not sure?"

"No. Maybe if he hadn't been wearing gloves."

"Tell me about the gloves."

"They were latex. The kind doctors wear." She hugged her arms across her middle and tried not to think about how his gloved hand had closed over her throat.

"How about his voice? Did he say anything?"

"He called me—" She broke off to take a deep breath. God. She didn't want to think about what that meant.

"What did he call you?" Jack prompted.

"Katydid," she answered softly. As she waited for his next question, she studied the glass of water she held. She was okay. She was in control. She was a big fat liar.

"Katydid? Is that a nickname?"

"Yes." She nodded. "Karen, my twin sister, gave it to me."

"Is she the only one who uses it?"

"My father did sometimes."

"Anyone else?"

She didn't want to say his name. Even inside her head,

she'd been avoiding it. Because saying the name aloud would make it too real.

"Katie, did anyone else call you by that name?" Chief Blade asked again, his voice still kind, but slightly louder this time. As if he thought the reason she'd failed to answer him was because she hadn't heard the question.

She nodded again. "Carlos Bricker. My ex-boyfriend. He'd use it to upset me."

"Why would it upset you?"

"My sister…she's dead."

He seemed to study her face. For the first time, she wondered what he saw when he looked at her. The side of her face ached from where she'd hit the wall. She was probably pretty bruised. When she talked, there was a searing pain on the left side of her lower lip, which probably meant it was busted.

What he saw…what anyone looking at her would see was the face of a victim. The demeanor of a victim. And she hated that even more than her physical appearance.

"Katie?"

For a second, she couldn't remember what they'd been talking about, then it came to her. About her sister. About the nickname.

"No one besides your family and Carlos knew about the nickname?" the police chief repeated.

She took another sip of water and hoped no one would notice her tears. "No." Admitting defeat, she wiped them off with her hands.

"When was the last time you saw Carlos?"

"A little over two months ago. I had just broken off the relationship and told him I was moving my paintings to another gallery. When I went to get them, he'd locked them up."

"What did you do?"

"I hired an attorney. But Carlos called later that same night. Evidently, my attorney had already contacted him. Carlos said that I'd regret my decision. I assumed he meant professionally." She took a deep breath. "Three nights later, he was waiting for me when I got home. I didn't see him until it was too late. I wouldn't have gotten out of my car if I had. He tried to drag me inside the condo. When a neighbor came out, Carlos took off. The neighbor never got a good look at him, though." She swallowed. "I filed charges. He produced a witness who said he was with her when the attack happened. The charges were dropped. I moved up here."

"So you believe Carlos Bricker hired someone to harm you?"

"Yes." She rubbed her forehead. Her head was really beginning to ache. Which wasn't a bad thing. If it hurt enough, she wouldn't be able to think anymore.

Chief Blade turned his attention to his brother. "Okay, Alec. What can you add to Katie's statement?"

"He's right-handed and knows how to handle a gun. Either military or police training, or maybe he's just heavy into weaponry. He placed two shots within inches of each other and over my head in a darkened house. Right-handed because of where he was standing at the time he fired and the trajectory of the rounds. My guess is a 9 mm auto. The fact he didn't panic suggests he's been in similar situations."

At that moment, the young deputy at the door let in a man dressed in jeans and a T-shirt emblazoned with the words Grateful Dead. He had a short, neatly trimmed and nearly black beard. A tape measure rode his belt and he carried a large leather case. Just inside the door, he stopped to pull paper covers over running shoes—the kind doctors and nurses used in the operating room—then looked toward the living room and his boss.

"Martinez, I think you know my brother," the police chief nodded at Alec, then motioned with a hand toward Katie. "This is Katie Carroll."

Katie managed a weak smile and received a nod from the young Hispanic man.

The police chief stood. "I'll have more questions, Katie, after I've had a chance to look around. We'll need the clothes you're wearing. I'll get you some to change into in a minute, but for now, try to relax. We'll try to get through here as fast as we can." He looked at his brother. "Perhaps you could get a list of anyone who may have been through the house recently. We're going to need to get their prints, too, for elimination."

He joined the technician in the foyer and they moved into the back hallway and the kitchen.

Alec sat in the chair Jack had vacated. "I know you said no to the hospital, but you really should go and get checked out." He reached out, pushed the hair away from her left cheek, his concerned eyes briefly studying the bruising. "I'd like to be able to tell you that it looks better than it feels, but I'm afraid the opposite is true." His smile was small, patient and fleeting. "You could have a minor concussion. And if nothing else, the doctor could give you something to help you sleep."

Sleep? She didn't think she'd be doing that anytime soon.

She struggled with a small smile of her own, one she intended to make her appear stronger than she was feeling. "I'm okay. Or will be when this is over."

"Shouldn't take much longer," he assured her, repeating his brother's words.

She nodded. "The idea that someone hates me enough to want me dead…" She shook her head slowly. "I think it would be easier if I was just in the wrong place at the wrong time. Because then I could tell myself that it had nothing to do with me."

She was starting to feel flat. As if she'd been up too long and was suffering from sleep deprivation. Able to function, but not very well.

Alec removed a small notepad from the inside pocket of his jacket. "It's just the adrenaline. It's not unusual to feel high one moment and then the next start to feel tired. Perhaps while you're still up to it, we should make that list of who's been inside the house."

She placed the glass of water on the table in front of her. "When you first busted in here, you yelled FBI."

"I was with the FBI. I'm not any longer." He didn't allow her to comment. "Who has access to your home?"

Because of the way he'd answered and how he seemed to want to brush by his past employment, she figured something had happened. That or he was anxious to fulfill his duties and leave. She wasn't looking forward to that moment.

"He was wearing gloves."

"But we can't be certain how long he'd been in the house. He may have removed them at some point."

She recalled the candlelight in her bedroom. Maybe he was right. Perhaps her attacker had removed his gloves to light them.

"Just the landlord. I think he hired an electrician to fix the electric panel box in the kitchen, but you'll need to check with him."

"We'll be asking him these same questions. How about friends? Coworkers?"

She lifted her gaze to his. "No. I've mostly kept to myself." Tonight was to have been the first foray into dating since she'd moved up here. She'd seen it as the beginning. A new start with new friends—a brand-new life where anything was possible. She liked Deep Water. Liked the people even more. They seemed less complicated than her Miami friends. More genuine.

She should have known it wasn't going to work.

Alec ripped out the page. "If you think of anyone else who's been through here, be sure to tell Jack."

When he started to stand, she stopped him with a hand on his jacket sleeve. "Thanks. For everything."

"You're welcome." He smiled, and this time his eyes seemed warmer. "For everything."

Her hand still rested on his arm. She was trying to work up the courage to ask him to stay with her for a few minutes more when Jack returned.

Self-conscious, she withdrew her hand, and as she did, Alec stood.

She swung her gaze toward Alec's brother. The police chief refused to meet it.

"Alec, you need to take a look at this."

"What is it?"

"It's the bedroom."

Katie started to get to her feet. Alec's hand resting on her shoulder kept her seated.

"Why don't you stay put for now?"

Chapter Three

Crime scene technician Andy Martinez stood in front of what Alec assumed to be the door to Katie's bedroom. He appeared to check the settings on the video camera he held. A 35 mm hung on his shoulder.

He glanced at his watch, and Alec wanted to ask him where he needed to be, but it wasn't any of his business. Maybe he had a hot date, or a wife to get home to. But the action reminded Alec that he'd also had other plans for tonight. He checked the time. Passengers would be embarking in twenty-five minutes, which meant he'd have to catch a flight in the morning.

"I'll shoot the video first, and then get the stills. Then bag up." Martinez pulled a large pad and a pencil from a side compartment of his case. "Anyone here want to do the sketch? I flunked first grade art. Never could get the arms and legs the same length on those stick figures."

He didn't know Martinez, but thought the kid seemed a bit nervous. As if something in the room had made him uncomfortable.

Jack motioned for Martinez to step away from the closed door. "That can wait a few minutes."

Alec looked at his brother, at the closed door Jack

stood in front of. "I take it you found something out of the ordinary?"

"Depends on which town you're in." With a grim expression, Jack nudged the door open.

Candlelight reached every corner of the small space. Not that anyone stepping inside would notice the candles, considering the rest of the room.

There were no pillows on the double bed, no top sheet, either. Just the fitted bottom sheet. The center of the bed was strewn with a path of red rose petals, as if flung there by a flower girl following a bride down the aisle. The remaining roses—at least two dozen—filled a vase on the dresser.

A seduction scene. If you could ignore the surgical tubing tied to the headboard. And the looped ends that could be quickly slipped around wrists and ankles, and which would only become tighter as the victim struggled. Since there was no footboard, the tubing had been attached to the legs of the Hollywood bed frame. Square knots, again, tied by a right-hander.

Three of the red rose petals had missed the bed entirely and resembled a blood trail.

Alec's gut twisted. Everything inside him wanted to deny what he was seeing. No one could look at the room and not be shaken by it. Not think about the woman who was to have been lashed down and terrorized. Murdered. It was what nightmares were made of. For Alec it was even more personal than that. It was the nightmare he couldn't escape. It represented not only the degradation that one human being could inflict upon another, it also represented Alec's own failure.

He stepped carefully into the room. One narrow path in and the same path out. He'd been working crime scenes for enough years that it had become second nature.

Without even counting, he knew there would be twenty-seven candles—the cheap variety, which accounted for the heavy scent of wax. Just as he knew the brand of box cutter on the nightstand—Swain. Just as he knew the picture over the bed had been removed to make room for a different kind of artwork.

The kind that required blood.

Eleven months ago, his flight into Philadelphia International had been delayed because of a snowstorm. When he'd landed, he'd thought about calling Jill, but she would have been sleeping. She was a teacher and got up early. The roads were a mess, and it had taken him seventy minutes to go twenty-eight miles. The house had been dark. He'd come in through the garage, stopped in the kitchen long enough to drink a glass of milk—his dinner—and to add kibble to the cat's dish.

He'd left his suitcase there, figuring he could undress in the dark and climb into bed without waking Jill. He'd thought the house cold, so had dialed up the thermostat as he passed.

He remembered that he'd hesitated at the bottom of the stairs, looked up into the familiar darkness above. He'd sensed something wasn't right, but had quickly written it off. He was just beat.

He'd taken only the first two steps when he'd smelled it…the heavy scent of blood. His grip on the railing tightening, he'd tried to convince himself he was wrong. That the smell of death had been with him for so many days he was no longer capable of breathing air that wasn't tainted with its stink.

And then he'd seen the bloody paw prints left by the cat.

Alec had taken the remaining steps two and three at a time, his weapon drawn.

But he was too late.

The attack had taken place midafternoon—the medical examiner had never been able to put an exact time on it because of the cool temperature in the house and the ceiling fan. Blood had soaked all the way through the mattress, forming a puddle on the wood floor beneath the bed.

"Alec." Jack had followed him into the room, and now interrupted the too-vivid memory. "Talk to me."

Talk to him? Alec realized he would give anything to talk to his brother. Not about police work and crime scenes, but about coming home, finding his wife murdered. To know deep down inside that he was the reason she was dead. That her death hadn't been the work of a sexual sadist, but of someone out to destroy Alec. Someone seeking revenge for some perceived wrong.

But he couldn't talk to Jack. Not because Jack wouldn't listen, but because Alec couldn't make himself say any of those words aloud.

"Alec?" This time Jack squeezed his brother's shoulder.

Alec stepped out from under what was meant to be a comforting gesture. The pink cotton rug deadened the sound of his hard soles. He looked down at the bed. At the blank wall above. In his mind, he saw the bloody message the killer had left him eleven months ago.

REMEMBER.

And he did remember. Every second of every day, he remembered.

Alec looked back at his brother, at the young crime scene tech Martinez. "He's grown tired of postcards. There's nothing visceral in paper and ink."

Stunned silence followed those words.

"But why now?" Jack remained unmoving.

It was as if the question threw some kind of switch inside Alec. He was no longer the grieving husband…desperate to right an unrightable wrong. He was the man who had spent years in the FBI facing the unimaginable. One of Quantico's best. In reality, he was beginning to believe that he wasn't all that much different from the men he'd hunted. Of late, he'd started to realize that he was more comfortable staring at photos of the dead than looking into the eyes of the living. He'd told his brother that tonight's date was just pizza and conversation, but it hadn't been. It had been a test. To see if he could sit across from an attractive woman and pretend that he was okay.

"Why now? Maybe he sees my leaving Philadelphia as a sign I'm moving on. He can't let that happen." Alec continued to examine the room, seeking subtle changes in the scene—a new twist—that might suggest that the killer was evolving.

Alec placed his hands in his pockets. For the first time in his career, they were shaking, not just with anger, but with fear, too. For the woman in the other room. He immediately closed out that line of thought, wouldn't allow himself to go there quite yet.

"He needs to maintain control. Control is very important to him. You can see it in the precision of everything he does." Alec checked out the top of the dresser, the room's small bookshelf. "He tidied up in here. Dusted. Rearranged her books. Probably went through them. He'd want to know everything he could about her." Not because he was interested in her, but because he wanted to know what had drawn Alec to her.

"How can you know that?" Martinez asked, his voice filled with skepticism.

Alec swung his gaze to the man briefly. "Because the

mantel in the living room hasn't been dusted recently. The end table showed signs that someone attempted to swipe away the worst of it with a hand, but didn't shift the lamp aside to be thorough—probably Katie when she got home tonight. Books are piled on the end of the sofa. The ones that fell onto the floor have been left there."

Alec closed his eyes in an attempt to stave off the headache building behind his right eye. "Living rooms are usually kept ready for company, but our bedrooms, that's where we can be ourselves. We can toss the magazine we've been reading in bed onto the floor, get up in the morning and step over it and never concern ourselves with the possibility that we're slobs." Several magazines were neatly stacked on the corner of the nightstand.

"And Katie?" Jack asked. "A waitress in a restaurant where you have breakfast? Why choose her?"

Alec thought back. "It's been suggested that I observe Katie more than other people. A few, including you, Jack, took it to mean that I had a romantic interest in her. Perhaps the UNSUB saw the same thing."

"He'd have to be damn close in order to do that," Jack said. There was a grimness in both the words and his tone.

Alec suspected his brother wasn't just thinking about tonight's assault. Jack was thinking about the monster who walked among them. What it meant for Deep Water.

Turning, Alec glanced at his brother first, and then Martinez. The look in the tech's eyes was wary now.

Alec had known it would eventually get out, the people in Deep Water would learn who he was. And once they did, they would look at him differently. Just as his coworkers had treated him differently when he'd returned to duty two months after he'd buried Jill. They were comfortable looking at the dead; accustomed to facing a victim's family. But when the victim was the spouse of one of their own? Well, that wasn't so easy for them. It forced them to recognize that they weren't any safer than the rest of the population. That their families were equally vulnerable. And if there was one thing no agent wanted to feel, it was pregnable.

"Any possibility it's a copycat?" Martinez asked.

Alec shrugged. "The scene's incomplete—no blood, no body—which leaves open the possibility of a copycat."

"But you don't think it is, do you?" Martinez asked.

"No. Even the best copycat killer usually makes a mistake with at least one of the props. The number of candles is the same, the brand of knife, the use of surgical tubing…"

CALMER NOW that she was alone, Katie set down the glass of water on the side table. What was it that the police chief wanted Alec to see in her bedroom? The candles?

She carefully tested her right cheek again, tracing the bone with only her fingertips. Yep. Still hurts. As did her neck and back and rib cage. And then there was her left knee. She flexed the joint to test it. Not as bad as it looked. Of course, come morning that might change.

Maybe Alec was right about the trip to the hospital. And after the hospital? What then? Where would she go?

She'd get a hotel room. There was no way she was staying in this house tonight or any other night. Maybe once the bruises faded, she'd fly out and see her parents, spend some time with them.

She was going to get her life back for real this time. Just as she had after her sister's death. It had taken some time and had been tough, but she'd done it. She was strong. That's what her father claimed. Karen may have been the bold one, but Katie was the one with the real strength in the family.

She glanced around the room. So why was she cowering here? Standing, Katie limped to the foyer entrance. She rubbed her arms compulsively, but it wasn't because she was cold. It was just the adrenaline still kicking around her system.

The front door was closed, but a breeze poured in through the broken glass of the upper portion. The young cop assigned to guard it stood with his back to her and didn't look in her direction.

She got as far as the kitchen before stopping. Glancing inside, she saw that the back door had been closed, but the chair she'd used to break the glass in the upper portion still hung there, two legs inside, two outside. She allowed her gaze to take in the rest of the room slowly. Streaks of red ran down the front of the painted cabinets. Wine, but for a brief moment it almost looked like blood.

For as long as she could, Katie fought the urge to glance over her shoulder, then, when the small hairs at the back of her neck had climbed to attention once more, she gave in to the need. Of course, she was the only one in the room. Drawing a cleansing breath, she decided that she had every right to be nervous. That it was a perfectly normal response to what she'd been through.

The sound and strobe of a camera flash prodded her back into the hallway and toward her bedroom. What was it that they were doing in there? How many photos could you take of candles? And then it occurred to her that maybe her attacker had come in through her bedroom window.

The scent of candle wax lingered still, a second one accompanied it. Something sweet. She frowned. Perfume? Flowers?

Another flare of light. She could see Martinez now, just inside the door, the camera aimed toward her bed. He wasn't talking, but she could hear the low murmurs of Alec and his brother. Martinez looked up when she was still five feet from the opening.

He lowered the camera. "Ma'am? You shouldn't—"

"What is it?"

She hadn't been able to see Alec from the hallway, but he managed to head her off before she could get to the door. He caught her by the shoulders and forced her backward, away from the door. His grip on her was firm but gentle. When their gazes met, she saw compassion in his eyes. She'd seen the same compassion two months ago in the eyes of the police officer who'd given her the news that the assault charges against Carlos were being dropped.

She tried to look past Alec's shoulder. Martinez was still taking pictures. What had happened in her bedroom?

She forced her gaze to meet his again. He looked troubled, the lines in his handsome face more pronounced. "It would be best if you waited in the living room."

"Best? This is my home." She tried to push past him again, but he blocked her. This time when their gazes met, the look in his eyes was cool, remote. Professional. Just like the cop two months ago when he'd explained how restraining orders rarely worked, that a self-defense course and a thirty-eight would be more effective when it came to protecting herself. She'd taken the course, but had refused to buy a gun.

"You shouldn't go in there, Katie. You have to trust me on that."

"Why? What's in there? What could be any worse than what has already happened to me tonight?" Even as she said it, she knew she wasn't being rational. If they were trying to keep her out, there was a reason. And that reason was that they didn't think she was strong enough to handle it.

She lifted her chin. "I'm not some weak female. If I was, I wouldn't be standing here. I'd be huddled out there on that couch where you left me." Raising her hands, breaking his hold on her, she backed away from him, and he let her go. "I've had a bad time of it. I admit that. But I'm strong enough to face whatever is in that room."

Though he continued to block her way, he suddenly looked very tired. Worried.

"Whatever is in there, Alec, can't be any worse than what's going through my mind right now."

His jaw hardened and the look in his eyes became one of unwilling acceptance. He wasn't happy about her insistence, but he would comply. "Are you sure, Katie? Really sure?"

"Yes." But she wasn't.

As Alec started to step past his brother, Jack stopped him. "She's been through an awful lot already."

"I know. But daylight won't make it any easier. It doesn't end for her here tonight. It's just the beginning."

Those confusing words echoed in her mind as she forced herself to take the final step.

The white candles were the first thing she saw—not the one or two she'd expected, but too many to count—and then the rose petals, splotches of blood spattered across snow. Katie backed away a half step. She didn't own white sheets. Had never owned a set. Which meant... Suddenly, she registered the plastic tubing tied to the headboard.

The trembling started deep inside. She hugged herself, her fingers digging into her arms. Images slammed through her. She was afraid to close her eyes, afraid if she did, she'd hear his voice again, calling her Katydid. Telling her that she was going to die.

Her knees weakened beneath her. She was shaking her

head slowly, as if in denial. She should have listened! Why hadn't she listened? As she turned to run, Alec caught her. Intent on escape, she shoved at his chest with her forearms, but he held on.

"Get out of my way!"

Instead of doing as she asked, he tightened his hold.

"I can't," he said softly, his voice raw with regret.

Not I won't, but I can't.

Suddenly she was holding on to him as she had in the kitchen, her fingers twisting into the fabric of his shirt, and then releasing their hold. Over and over and over again. As they had earlier, after several seconds, his arms tightened around her, and she found herself locked against his hard body, listening to the steady beat of his heart.

But all she could think about was the room behind her. How if Alec hadn't asked her out tonight, or had been running late, she might be already dead.

"Come on." He helped her out to the living room, sat her back down on the couch. The last time he'd sat her here, she'd thought her problems couldn't get any worse. She'd been wrong.

When he passed it to her, she numbly took the freshly filled water glass, but just held it in her hands, rotating it as if she were suddenly blind and searching desperately for a Braille message on its surface. Some answer as to why this was happening to her.

How had she managed to get herself mixed up with a man like Carlos Bricker? She was cautious where people were concerned—especially since Karen's death—and her instincts were usually pretty good. So how had Carlos managed to fool her so completely?

And more importantly, why hadn't he come himself? If he hated her that much, why send someone? She thought she knew why, though. If she turned up dead, Carlos was bound to be a prime suspect. But then again, his new girlfriend might be willing to give him an alibi for the attempted assault of his ex-girlfriend. Carlos could be very charming and persuasive; he could easily convince the new girlfriend that the ex was just out to get him. But when it came to a murder charge, she might not be so willing to provide an alibi. Because new girlfriends eventually became ex-girlfriends. And what went around came around.

She didn't look up when Alec sat in the chair facing her. She'd told him she was tough. That she could take whatever was in that room. Well, she wasn't quite that strong.

Katie rubbed her forehead as if the action could erase what she'd seen. It wouldn't. She suspected she'd be seeing that room in her nightmares for many years to come. Maybe for the rest of her life.

"How much money does it take to buy…to buy someone to do this?" She rotated the glass faster now. It was a stupid question really, but she still found herself wondering what it had cost the creep. Recently, he'd had money problems, so maybe he had even sold some of her paintings to pay for the hit on her.

"Your ex-boyfriend has nothing to do with what happened here tonight."

It took a second for his words to sink in. When they did, she raised her gaze to his for the second time in seconds. "What are you saying?"

"This nickname. Katydid. Is there anything in your bedroom that has that written on it? The back of a photo? Inscribed on something in your jewelry box? In a book?"

She looked down at her hands, at the dried blood beneath her nails and at the sterling ring on her right hand.

She fingered the band. Her sister had given it to her only weeks before her death. The inside was inscribed: *To Katydid, My better half.* It was the only piece of jewelry she owned with an inscription, and she never removed it.

"Maybe the back of a photo." She tightened her grip on her hands. "But I don't understand… Who else would want to harm me?" And then she saw it in Alec's eyes. "You know who it is? Who did that to my room?" How was that possible?

"Yes." He was composed. Too composed. Guarded.

"But how can you know who it is?"

Exhaling sharply, he looked away. When he looked back, his expression was even grimmer. "Eleven months ago, while I was still with the Bureau, I came home after two weeks on the road and found my wife murdered. Our bedroom looked exactly like yours does tonight."

What was he saying? That the man who had killed his wife wanted to kill her? But why? That made no sense. She was shaking with the effort not to cry. Her fingers curled into her arms as she continued to fight for control.

"Why? Why would he come here to kill me?" Of course, she could guess.

Still seated in the chair facing her, Alec held his face in his hands for several seconds, and then, letting out a harsh breath, looked at her again.

Jack walked in at that moment and placed her jewelry box on the coffee table. The box wasn't the department store variety, but a hand-painted wooden one done by an artist friend. A small chameleon peeked out from beneath the huge red hibiscus bloom covering the top. Now the outside of the box was covered in what looked like copier toner.

Alec slipped on latex gloves before lifting the lid with the end of a pen.

There was a small wad of tip money on top. Probably

seventy or eighty dollars at most. He carefully lifted it by the edges and placed it in a plastic bag.

He looked at her. "I need you to go through and tell me if anything is missing."

Still reeling from what he'd told her, she took the ballpoint he passed. Her fingers were shaking, but with some effort, she managed to steady them.

She had very few pieces of expensive jewelry. An aquamarine ring her parents had given her for her sixteenth, the expensive watch she'd purchased when one of her paintings had finally brought more than a thousand dollars, the gold bracelet her dad had surprised both Katie and her mom with on Valentine's Day two years before.

She lined them up next to the box. The only other worthwhile piece was the locket. It was usually tangled up in the bird nest at the bottom of the box. She rooted around. When was the last time she'd seen it? She'd worn the gold bracelet last week and the necklace had been here then. She could feel the pressure building in her chest, the sense of her confusion spreading. It had to be here.

In desperation, she used the pen to lift out the wad of cheap necklaces and bracelets. The jewelry landed noisily on the table next to the box.

"Katie?"

"It has to be here!"

"What has to be?"

Calm down. "A locket. It belonged to my grandmother."

"Any chance you mislaid it?"

"No." She shook her head. She could feel her palms begin to go clammy. "I only wear it when I get dressed up, and I haven't since I came here." She'd planned to wear it tonight. On their date.

Why the locket and not the more valuable bracelet?

How could her attacker have known which item meant the most to her?

She lifted her gaze to meet Alec's. "Was there something... Did he take a piece of your wife's jewelry?"

Alec nodded.

Chief Blade had been standing near the fireplace, but now broke in. "Maybe you should let me take things from here, Alec," he said quietly. He sat on the opposite end of the couch. "I think at this point the best thing we can do is find you someplace safe. Is there someone you can stay with? Family? Friends?"

She hadn't wanted her parents to see her bruised up. Hadn't wanted to worry them. But given the situation, did she have a choice? She could stay with friends, but that would mean returning to Miami. And even if Carlos hadn't hired someone to kill her, she wasn't ready to chance running into him quite yet.

"My parents are out west. They're in a motor home. Arizona, Utah—I don't know where exactly because they've been moving around a lot. I suppose I could go out and..."

Alec interrupted. "He'll just follow."

Jack shot a look at his brother. "But if he doesn't know where she is—"

Alec cut him off. "How long do you think it will take him to find out? You'll just be putting additional people at risk."

Katie looked at both men. "I won't do anything that puts my parents or anyone in danger."

"Okay." Chief Blade glanced at Alec. "What do you suggest, then?"

"Twenty-four hour protection in a safe house."

"For how long?"

Irritation flashed in Alec's face, and his jaw hardened. "For as long as it takes."

"Hell, Alec, we're a small force. We don't have the budget to cover that type of protection. The best move is to get her out of town."

Alec rubbed the back of his neck. "There is no place safe." Alec took a deep breath in an obvious effort to hold on to his temper. "This isn't about Katie. It's about control. Of me. If he lets her get away, he'll have lost control. He can't allow that to happen."

She'd been numbly listening, but now stood on shaky legs. "I still…I still don't understand. Why me?" She realized just how weak and whiny the question sounded, but she was beyond caring.

"Because," Alec said, "he believes I have a romantic interest in you."

"That's ridiculous. We haven't even gone out on a date."

"Very true. But that wasn't what it looked like two weeks ago when I had forgotten my wallet and you covered my breakfast check."

"And you came back an hour later with money and daisies," she added. This couldn't be happening. Not to her.

Chief Blade looked at Martinez, who had just shown up at the foyer door. "I'm through in the bedroom. Now might be a good time to get the fingernail clippings and scrapings for DNA testing. And then we'll let you go change out of what you're wearing."

Martinez made quick work of obtaining the samples while the other men watched. Standing, he again picked up his case. "I'll go get started on the kitchen."

Martinez started to turn away, and then stopped. "If you're looking for a safe house, I just moved into a new place. Last owner was a security freak. This guy wouldn't have any reason to look for her out there."

The police chief seemed to consider the suggestion.

"Okay. Perkins, Jamison and Thompson are backups. I want all four of you staying out there. At least for tonight."

IT WAS WELL AFTER one in the morning when Alec and Jack sat down in Jack's office. Deep Water's police department, which was composed of nineteen commissioned officers and six non-com support staff, had recently moved into a renovated building, dating back to the turn of the century.

When most towns in Central Florida's Cougar County were plowing down the buildings that reflected their mediocre start, Deep Water had embraced its heritage of cattle barons and citrus kings. Buildings that had been ready to fall down were shored up, restored. Layers of asphalt were removed from downtown streets to reveal the worn but beautiful bricks beneath.

The Big Freeze of 1895 had run off most of the citrus industry, but even today, cattle grazed on much of the land outside the city limits. The feed store, which still occupied a prime chunk of ground at the center of town, maintained a hitching rail, and it wasn't unusual to see a cow pony tied there early in the morning.

A modern town with grace and integrity. And now a monster.

Alec slumped back in the chair, and, resting his head against the wall, closed his eyes. Without aspirin, the headache had gotten worse. A good night's sleep usually took care of it, but he doubted he'd be getting one of those anytime soon.

He'd already supplied his fingerprints for comparison to those found in the house, as had Katie.

Jack propped his elbows on the desk. "I'll send an officer around to get elimination fingerprints from the landlord. The evidence will go to the lab in the morning. Including the shoe cast."

A fairly clear footprint had been found just outside the kitchen door. But even if it belonged to Katie's attacker, it would have little value until they had a suspect in custody.

Deep Water didn't have a laboratory of its own, so the evidence would be sent to the Florida Department of Law Enforcement's lab in Daytona Beach for analysis. Alec didn't expect them to come back with anything useful. This wasn't the kind of killer who made mistakes.

"I should have seen this coming," he said quietly. "I should have recognized the probability Jill's killer would follow me to Deep Water. Nothing but damned arrogance on my part."

"You always were arrogant. Even in high school and college. It's what made you good." Jack studied him. "As far as the rest, we all make mistakes."

Alec scrubbed his face. "Not the kind that cost women their lives."

Jack popped open a can of iced tea. After several long swallows, he set it aside. "But she's okay. We just need to figure out how to keep her that way." Jack stirred the dish of hard candies on the credenza behind him. He'd quit smoking several months ago, and now satisfied his oral fixation with cherry drops.

Jack tossed the wrapper toward the trash can. "With that in mind, maybe it's time we start being honest with each other."

"I wasn't aware that we weren't."

"You're right. It's not really a matter of honesty, is it? It's more a matter of letting it all hang out. Saying not only the easy things, but also the hard ones. We've never done that. We Blades aren't really made that way, are we?"

"No," Alec agreed. "Maybe you should tell me what it is you want me to be honest about."

Jack leaned forward. "Is there another reason you might want to keep Katie in town?"

"Keeping her alive would seem like a good enough reason for most people."

Jack nodded. "Yes, it would. But so does nailing the man who murdered Jill."

"What are you talking about?" But he knew.

"It's been eleven months, Alec. And we both know the stats. The longer a homicide goes unsolved, the less likely charges will be brought." Rising, he paced to the window. "I've seen it in your eyes. You're not so much tormented by Jill's death as you are by the possibility that you may never catch this guy. You've helped put hundreds of his kind behind bars, but you can't get this one. It eats you up inside. So much so that you might be willing to grab on to anything to turn the odds in your favor."

Jack faced him. "And then suddenly you have it. Bait."

Alec's right hand curled into a fist over the arm chair. "You're right. All of what you've said is true. Even the fact that I'm desperate enough to use any advantage. But do you really think I would place an innocent woman at risk?"

When his brother remained silent, Alec had his answer. "Well, you're wrong. I have one woman's death on my conscience. I couldn't handle a second. And maybe you need to ask yourself how well you're going to sleep if you cut her loose and he does go after her. If she winds up dead. Who would be the cold SOB then?"

Alec got to his feet. "Katie Carroll is in extreme danger. Get another opinion. Call Seth Killian. He'll tell you the same thing. You fail to give her protection, and you might as well stake her to the ground like a sacrificial lamb."

Jack looked up at his brother. "Call Seth? Your *friend* at the FBI? I guess I should trust his opinion. After all you two *are* tighter than *brothers*."

Alec knew he should never have brought up Seth's name. "Call whoever you want, just don't put her on the next bus out of here without consulting someone else first."

Jack studied him. "You're that sure?"

"Yes." Alec nodded. "I'm that sure."

Chapter Four

Katie glanced at the cell phone sitting just to the right of the laptop computer. The phone was still on, and the battery charge was okay.

So why wasn't it ringing?

A pervasive sense of loneliness, of disconnection from the real world had settled over her.

After only three days, Martinez's guest bedroom had become her jail cell. A nine-by-twelve iron lung that kept her alive, but at the same time kept her trapped. And she felt numb—at least mentally—from lack of outside stimuli. Fresh air. Sounds of birds, of traffic, of the wind. Emotionally numb, too. She realized she was spending too much time worrying about things beyond her control.

She paced from desk to bed, plopped down on the edge and stared at the bedroom door. For the past few nights, Alec had called by eight thirty.

At first, she'd thought it was guilt that prompted the calls, and perhaps there was some of that involved, but she now suspected there was a deep-seated kindness in Alec. And that he understood more than most what she was going through and wanted to help in any way he could.

But, she admitted, it really didn't matter why he called.

She'd come to look forward to their conversations. And there was so little for her to look forward to.

Except perhaps the news that her attacker had been caught. That it was over. That she could go home.

Out in the living room, Martinez and the other two cops cranked up the television volume loud enough that the floor pulsed with the sound of Monday Night Football.

She could be watching the game with Martinez and his cop friends. But being around Martinez made her feel like a victim. It was in the way he looked at her sometimes and in the way he carefully chose words, and even in his choice of television shows.

Last night after dinner, he'd turned on a movie—a sappy, made-for-television romance, complete with guardian angels. He'd sat through all two hours, eyes wide-open and glazed with boredom. And she'd been feeling petty enough that she'd let him.

A loud round of raucous laughter propelled her to her feet. How much longer could she go on like this without going completely crazy?

Flicking on the computer again, she accessed the Internet. She'd read most of what there was to offer on the only subjects that interested her: serial killers and the FBI's legendary behavioral scientist, Alec Blade. The man who had brought down the infamous Columbus Butcher. The man who had helped the Richmond Police Department solve the Railroad Killings. The man who had walked away from his career when his wife was murdered.

She'd made herself read the newspaper articles from the days and weeks following Jill Blade's death. For some reason she'd thought it would help. Instead, they had only fueled nightmares that didn't fade in the light of day.

She had just reached Babs Lacey's interview with Alec

for a segment on the real-life hero behind a recent prime-time television hit when the cell phone vibrated on the desk. Katie grabbed the phone.

"Hey, there." She somehow made her greeting sound casual.

"Hello, there, yourself." Alec's voice was pitched low and smooth. Soft jazz played in the background, the lonely, lazy sound of a sax. Additional sounds like that of rain battering a windshield told her that he was in his car.

"You're not home yet?"

"No. I was stopping off for some dinner first."

"I thought you had a gourmet kitchen. And liked to cook."

"I do. But it's been a long day, and it's a miserable night." She could hear just how tired he was.

The nights were always the worst for her. Unending. Empty of everything but the fear.

Her fingers tightened on the phone, and she found herself glancing at Alec's face on the screen. The image was from a year ago, and yet he looked far younger. Invincible. The chiseled mouth smiling with an ease she'd never witnessed in the weeks and months that he'd been coming into the diner, and the look in his dark eyes was confident and happy.

The interview had taken place only weeks before the murder.

"How'd it go in Philadelphia?" He'd told her he needed to fly up today, but hadn't elaborated. As much as they talked about other things, they never discussed what had happened to his wife. Or even her sister. It was as if they both appreciated the other's boundaries.

"The suspect's lawyer's demanding a deal on the table before he'll give up anything. I think he actually may know something, if we can get him to talk." She could hear the frustration in his voice, and it made her realize that for her it had been only three days, but for him it had been far longer.

Over the past few days, with so much time to dwell on so few topics, she'd found herself analyzing what it was that had attracted her to Alec in the first place. Beyond a face that was both interesting and handsome and a lean, hard body that had been molded by years of running. She'd decided it was his quiet control that had made her say yes when he suggested dinner. Because after Carlos, quiet, calm control had made her feel safe.

"Did you get the package?" Alec asked, dragging her up and out of her own thoughts.

"Yes. Thanks. I hope it wasn't too awkward, but I didn't know who else to ask." He'd done some shopping for her. Shorts and shirts, panties, bras. It was the first time she'd ever given a man her bra and panty size, and his choices had surprised her. Perhaps they weren't quite thongs, but some of the panties were barely there.

When the police had released the crime scene, Alec had sent over some of her clothes from the house, but she'd continued to live in the same T-shirt and running shorts Martinez had lent her that first night.

Katie stood and paced. "I know it's ridiculous, but I just couldn't wear anything of mine. Just the idea that he might have touched them. It gave me the creeps."

"It's understandable."

"Is it?" To her, her behavior seemed irrational. They were just clothes. Even if her attacker had touched them, after the half dozen trips they'd made through the washer, nothing of him could remain. But her skin had crawled each time she'd tried to put them on. In the end, she'd stuffed them in the trash.

A loud whoop came from the other room, closely

followed by, "Get in there! Get in there!" Then more male screams of frustration.

Katie turned her back on the noise as if to shut them out. "Thanks for the DVDs, too." He'd included half a dozen movies—all comedies—as if he'd known she couldn't watch anything else right now. Certainly not the psychological thrillers she normally enjoyed.

"You're welcome. What's with the toothpicks, though?"

The tightness in Katie's middle eased. "Martinez has been teaching me Five Card Stud and Texas Draw. I ran out of pennies after my first lesson." She'd never been fond of cards, but by the second day she'd been ready to try anything to distract herself. She suspected Martinez had felt pretty much the same way.

"Are you any good?" Alec asked.

"At cards? Sure." She pushed her hair off her forehead. "Good enough to know when my opponent is palming aces." Having reached the bed, she sat.

"Martinez cheats for toothpicks?"

"I think it has more to do with the male ego than toothpicks. And right now, given the situation, I like the idea that he hates to fail at anything." Another slight pause. But the lulls in conversation no longer felt uncomfortable.

"How are you and Martinez making out?"

"Better. But he needs a night off." *I need a night off.*

"He's supposed to be on sick leave. If he's seen out on the town, his cover is blown."

"At least he's got some company tonight. A couple of cop buddies came by to watch the game."

The aroma of popcorn leaked through the walls, along with more male shouts.

"Maybe you should try painting or something. I could get some art supplies sent over, a few canvases, that type of thing. Or if you were already working on something, I could probably find some way to get it to you."

"I don't want anything from that house."

"What about photo albums? Personal items? Knick-knacks?"

She rubbed her forehead. He was right. There were some things—those with a history that was unrelated to what had happened—that she'd want. Her fingers tightened on the phone. "I prefer not to think about it right now."

There was a long pause in the conversation where only the sound of jazz came through the phone before Alec turned down or flicked off the radio. "Did you call and talk to your parents?"

"Yes, I phoned them and gave them this number to reach me. But I didn't tell them, and I don't plan to. Not yet."

Another pause as if he weighed words. "Do you want me to contact them?"

"No. Given the circumstances, that wouldn't be such a good idea."

Silence stretched. She knew what Alec was thinking because her own mind had traveled the same roads. Numerous times she had tried to blame him for what had happened, but had always come back to the fact that he was even more a victim than she was. She had simply been unlucky enough to be in the wrong place at the wrong time.

"Do you think that's wise?"

"Look, Alec. I just don't want to worry them. If I tell them, they'll be on the next plane back here, and there's absolutely nothing they can do."

"How do you think they'll feel when they find out that you didn't tell them?"

"I'd rather deal with their anger later than their fear right now. I've got enough of my own to deal with."

The pitch of his voice dropped lower with his next words. "How are you doing?"

Had Martinez passed along that she was having night-mares where she woke up screaming? Glancing at the door Martinez kicked in that first night and spent most of the second day repairing, she massaged her forehead and tried to think of a suitable reply.

"Katie?"

"Not so fine," she answered finally. She took a deep breath and let it out slowly. What was wrong with her? It wouldn't do either of them any good for her to be honest. "But I'll be okay."

"You will be," he agreed. "When this is over."

She'd used those same words the night of the attack. She'd believed them then, but now she didn't.

Katie shifted the small phone to a more comfortable position. "Any news?"

"They've been able to match up most of the finger-prints to people who had a legitimate reason to be in the house. There weren't any prints on the candles. The utility—" A long silence followed.

He was choosing his words carefully just as Martinez did. Afraid that she would fall apart on him otherwise. "Damn it, Alec, don't you treat me like I can't handle anything. I get enough of that around here. You were about to say that there were no prints on the utility knife?"

"Yes. And they're still waiting on DNA results from the nail clippings."

"But even if they're successful," Katie said, "even if some of the blood or skin cells belong to him, unless he's committed a crime and his profile's in CODIS…"

God. Listen to her. She was speaking in acronyms. CODIS was the FBI's Combined DNA Index System, a national database capable of matching offenders to crimes. Up until a few days ago, if someone had asked her what CODIS stood for, she would have had a better chance of guessing winning lottery numbers.

The phone silence stretched long enough this time that she'd thought they'd been cut off. "Alec?"

"Martinez should keep his damn mouth shut." There was an edge to his tone.

"He has." She glanced down at the red carpeting. "Your brother lent me a computer. I've been looking around on the Internet."

After several seconds, she stopped pacing and, leaning against the door, closed her eyes. Maybe ignorance was bliss. Maybe if she hadn't discovered what she had about murder investigations and how they worked, about the percentages of murders that were actually solved, she could buy into the idea that her attacker would be apprehended.

"You shouldn't be doing that," Alec said.

"What should I be doing? It isn't as if I have anything else to do with my time." Katie pushed away from the door. "I need to know, Alec. I ask your brother, and he gives me vague answers. I ask Martinez and he changes the subject. I ask you…"

"And I avoid telling you the truth because I don't want you to worry."

"Well, it's not working. I know you're trying to be… what?" She fumbled for the right word. "Gallant? But it's my life. I need to know. I need to make plans."

"What kind of plans?"

"What I'll do if he isn't apprehended."

"It won't come to that. I promise."

She took a deep, steadying breath, and then let it out slowly. "You can't make that promise, Alec. No one can."

Chapter Five

Alec closed the cell phone, ending the call to Katie. He'd known it was going to be hard on her. What he hadn't known was how he would react to the fear in her voice. He shoved a hand through his hair in frustration that he was no closer to getting her attacker. Jill's killer.

Fingerprinting analysis had been completed, those prints not eliminated as belonging to people who had been in the house for legitimate reasons run through the Automatic Fingerprint Identification System. There had been no matches. He hadn't really expected any.

Which meant what they had left was a cast of a shoe print—size ten and hard-soled—some fibers that had been found during the casting, and the fingernail clippings. The shoe cast was of little value until they had a suspect, and the lab had yet to process the other two. Even with Jack pushing, it could take upwards of a month to get DNA results.

Alec pulled into the crowded parking lot of Crabby Joe's. Because of its location near the interstate, the sports bar drew both a local crowd and those heading across state. He wasn't a big football fan and usually steered clear on Monday nights. But tonight he didn't want to go home to a silent house where he'd be alone with his thoughts.

Alec turned off the key and just sat there, no longer trying to hide from the pain. Why was it that, even with Jill's constant dropping of hints, he'd never been able to remember their wedding anniversary—the day they'd become one? But he couldn't seem to forget the day he'd lost her. The anniversary of her death. There was something wrong with that, wasn't there?

Rain speckled the windshield in slow drops. A truck pulled into the lot as he stepped from the black sport utility, the vehicle's headlights slashing across the front of the building, then bouncing as a tire dropped into a washout. Alec waited until a man and a woman climbed out and headed inside before he locked up and followed them in.

At the last moment, with his hand already reaching for the bar's front door, he glanced over his shoulder. He didn't see anyone, but for the past two days he hadn't been able to shake the feeling he was being stalked. Maybe Jill's killer thought he'd be stupid enough, careless enough, to lead him to Katie.

It was exactly what Alec hoped for. That eventually the killer's level of frustration when he couldn't locate Katie would build to the point he would make a mistake.

He scanned the parked cars. It took everything in him not to search each and every one of them—the foolish behavior of those first weeks and months following the murder that had earned him a medical leave. The same crazy behavior that made him walk away from the only thing he was truly good at. Tracking monsters.

With one final look over his shoulder, he went inside.

The dark bar was crowded with nine-to-fivers who had stripped off their suit coats, tourists wearing either shorts or brightly patterned shirts and workers from local ranches and citrus groves. The noise level ebbed and flowed in unison with the televised football game.

Florida had banned smoking in public places, but the scent of stale cigarettes lingered like a seasoned panhandler on a promising corner.

Finding a table at the back, where a small enclave of diehards watched a television tuned to around-the-clock news, he pretended to scan a menu while he checked out the other diners. The couple at the next table discussed their day at a local theme park and their coming trip home. From the woman's accent, he placed them as tourists from New Hampshire, now headed back north. Two well-dressed men sat at the table next to them. He eavesdropped for several seconds on their discussion of the recent stock market climb, the lazy flow of their consonants and vowels suggesting coastal Georgia.

Every time the front door opened, Alec managed to get a look at whoever entered. So far, no one appeared to be looking for someone in the crowd. But there was no reason for the killer to come inside. He could sit out there and wait for Alec to leave.

He'd already placed his food order and taken his first taste of the double bourbon when he spotted his brother, still in uniform, just inside the door. In turn, having located him, Jack made his way through the crowded tables.

Dropping into the chair across from Alec, he glanced at the tall drink. "Never seen you drink the hard stuff."

"You should have been around three years ago." Alec saluted his brother before taking a deep sip. "I was a real pro."

Jack placed his cell phone on the table. "What happened?"

"To make me start?"

Jack leaned back. "No. What made you stop?"

Alec put the drink down, ran a finger up the cool, smooth surface of the glass. "Jill made me see what I was doing." He'd been working an especially horrific case at the time, a series of child abductions, and had convinced himself that he needed the anesthetic of alcohol to cope.

Jack studied him with sharp gray eyes. "So what are you doing now?"

"Unwinding."

"Are you sure that's all?"

"Yeah." Alec pushed the drink away, suddenly realizing that the drink in front of him was all the evidence he needed that he wasn't quite as detached as he should be. That just maybe he'd allowed Katie Carroll to get a bit too close.

He needed to stay sharp and focused. It wasn't just about justice anymore, or even about the revenge of those first few months. A woman's life was at stake now. And because he didn't like the idea that his brother was seeing a little too deeply into his psyche, he asked, "Are you ordering?"

"No."

Alec wondered why he hadn't picked up on Jack's body language sooner. The stiff shoulders, the hands resting clasped on the tabletop. Only they weren't resting, were they? Jack suddenly tapped the table with his right hand three or four times in a nervous gesture, then shifted in his chair.

Something was up, and from what Alec was seeing, he figured it was bad news. "Did some of the lab results come back?"

"No. State lab is still working with a backlog. I put some more oil on the fire, but it'll probably be another few days before we hear anything."

"Missing Atlanta and all those resources you had at your disposal?" Alec asked. "Three days for ballistic results? Only a few more to get DNA?"

"You only need the facilities if you have the crime load to warrant it. And Deep Water doesn't." Several times, Alec had suggested Jack come work with him. There was enough business, and the money was a helluva lot better than police work, but Jack wasn't interested. Initially, Alec had believed it was because his brother didn't want to work with him, but Alec had finally come to realize that wasn't it at all. Jack liked police work. So Alec had quit asking.

"So what's on your mind?"

"Besides having a killer on the loose in my town?" Jack pointed to the closest television. He motioned the bartender to ease up the volume. "And senate hopeful Paul Darby?"

Turning around more fully so he could see the screen, Alec recognized Jolie Kennedy, WKMG's attractive brunette reporter. She stood in front of the Orange County Police Department, all five foot three inches of her.

"…Hate mail isn't anything new for senate candidate Paul Darby." The politician's familiar face flashed on the screen. "But even Mr. Darby was shocked by what one of his campaign assistants found in a package addressed to the politician. The nine-foot rattlesnake, indigenous to Florida, had been mutilated. There was also a typewritten threat included in the package, but law enforcement is withholding the contents of that note." In the background, two deputies held up the snake, obviously not for the benefit of the onlookers, but in the course of their investigation.

The reporter continued, "But those in Paul Darby's camp are suggesting that this latest special delivery may be another effort by pro-development groups afraid that Darby's tough environmental stance could slow Florida's growth, and their ability to make a living."

Again, the reporter glanced over her shoulder as the officers boxed up the dead reptile. "Rallies in both Fort Myers and Clewiston have ended in arrests. Only this week, Darby's manager suggested that the recent incidents may lead the politician to bypass several stops on his campaign trail."

Alec's eyes narrowed as he considered not just the a story, but the man it was about.

"Do you know Darby?" Jack asked.

"Only as the man who put Benito Binelli behind bars." Alec pushed the unfinished bourbon away. Stuff tasted like waterlogged cigarettes. He glanced around the dim interior. Or maybe it was just the atmosphere. Or his mood. Home was starting to look more appealing than the crowded sports bar.

Jack refocused his attention on Alec. "If Darby has any sense, he'll bypass Deep Water."

"Any chance of that happening?"

"Sure." Jack gave a weak grin. "About the same as my finding a blonde in my bed when I get home tonight. A town like Deep Water has more environmentalists than wealthy builders, so he'll show. Unfortunately, it appears as if some of the large developers in the state have banded together and are paying people to disrupt his rallies. If Darby shows up here, there's a good possibility that there will be trouble."

"But then," Alec said, "as Dade County's toughest prosecutor, Darby's used to trouble, isn't he? And so are you."

"But this town isn't." Leaning back, Jack scrubbed his face.

Alec saw the fatigue in his brother's eyes and felt badly. His moving here wasn't supposed to have caused Jack problems, but it had.

"So why were you looking for me?" Alec asked his brother.

"Since you're footing the bill for Katie's protection, I thought I should talk to you first."

"What about?"

"Some changes need to be made."

He'd been expecting this since Katie mentioned Martinez's cabin fever. Alec blew out a breath of frustration. "He wants out, doesn't he?"

Jack shook his head. "Not even close. I checked the personnel files. He's used up his personal days and paid vacation. I have one man going out this week and another just busted a leg this morning. Which means I have to have him back on shift by the day after tomorrow or risk losing *my* job."

"That doesn't give me much time to find a replacement and make arrangements for moving her."

"Martinez isn't any happier about this." Jack reached across and took a sip of Alec's abandoned bourbon. "I hear from some of the guys who have been hanging out with him that he's fallen for her."

Alec felt a small jab of irritation. "He should know better than to allow that to happen."

Jack lowered the glass, but his gaze remained speculative. "Most men can't just turn it on and off like a faucet."

Actually, it was just a matter of training. Observe, but don't get involved. Jill had claimed he had the technique down pat, and until tonight, he'd thought so, too.

Reclaiming the bourbon, Alec finished it in two large gulps. "I'll make the arrangements."

"Still determined to keep her in town?"

"In a big city, he'd have no problem blending in. In Deep Water, it won't be so easy. He'll make a wrong move, and someone will see it."

"Maybe he isn't even here anymore. Maybe he decided it was too dangerous. At least for the moment."

"He's here." Alec glanced at the occupants of the tables before allowing his gaze to wander in a casual manner to the bar where football fans sat elbow to elbow with one another. Even in the dimness, he could see the reflections of their faces in the mirror. They'd all been sitting there when he'd walked in.

And then, just as Alec was about to look away, he saw a movement in the mirror, a face, caught briefly, a gaze locked with his for the most transitory of moments—there and then gone. Not someone at the bar, though. Someone moving through the dining room.

Standing, he scanned the room. A large group of men and women stood near the exit, saying their good-nights. Four men at a nearby table laughed loudly. Three servers moved among the tables, one taking orders, the other two loaded with full trays of meals.

"What is it?" Jack asked, still sitting.

Alec sank back in his chair. "Nothing."

ALEC CLIMBED out of bed at six on Tuesday morning, nearly tripping over the black cat stretched out on the pine floor beside the bed. He gave the animal a look that would have made most academy trainees and suspects nervous, but the cat merely lifted his head enough to look at him and, squinting because of the room's sudden brightness, yawned.

Jill had acquired the cat from one of her students, and Alec had quickly nicknamed him the Black Demon. Now, eleven months after Jill's memorial, the cat slept in his room, oftentimes even on the bed with him. Alec tried to tell himself that he tolerated the cat merely because Jill had loved the animal, but he knew better.

He pulled on jogging shorts and a T-shirt, strapped on a

pair of running shoes in preparation for his usual six-mile run out at Deep Water Springs. He did his standard fifty push-ups and twice that many crunches, then headed downstairs.

He had barely made the coffee and placed a bowl of food on the floor in front of the expectant cat when the buzzer at the front gate sounded. Checking the closed-circuit monitor on the kitchen counter and seeing a police vehicle, he pushed the button to open the wrought-iron gates.

What would bring Jack by at this time of morning? Unless he wanted to know if Alec had made arrangements for Katie. Which he had. He'd been up until two in the morning tracking down and procuring one of the top personal-protection men in the country. The man hadn't come cheap, but he was between jobs and willing to travel on short notice.

Alec poured coffee for himself and Jack. His right index finger looped through the handles of both mugs, he answered the door.

Instead of his brother, though, Katie stood there, with Martinez right behind her.

He frowned. "You shouldn't be here."

"We need to talk," she said. Not waiting for an invitation, she stepped inside.

Martinez tried to follow, but Alec caught him in the middle of his chest with an open palm. "What in the hell possessed you to bring her here of all places?"

Martinez eyes met his. Alec could see the other man's irritation. But it was nothing compared to what he could feel in the man's tense muscles. And nothing compared to the anger Alec was feeling at the moment.

"Look, man, she threatened to call a cab if I didn't bring

her. She found out I was going back to work and that you were making other arrangements for her."

"So you just let her call the shots?"

"What was I supposed to do? Hog-tie her?"

"If you had to." In spite of his words, Alec dropped his hand and, passing Martinez a cup of coffee, motioned him inside. He had planned to move Katie from Martinez's place directly to her new quarters, but in some ways her appearance here this morning might not be a bad thing. Let the UNSUB get a look at her and begin to believe that he almost had her. Then move her beyond his reach. The UNSUB they chased wouldn't be able to handle it. It would put him one more step closer to making a mistake.

When he turned around, Katie stood in the large central hallway facing him. Looking at her—at the silky, dark hair, at the soft mouth, at the intense, gray eyes—was almost like taking a quick jab just below the belt, the kind of blow that weakened your knees and left you fighting for a deep breath. All he could seem to think about was that the loose rugby shirt and baggy shorts concealed size five bikini panties and size 34-B breasts, and left exposed long, athletic legs.

Not exactly the observation of an uninvolved special agent. But then he wasn't an agent anymore. He was a civilian. Which didn't change the fact that he shouldn't be thinking about how perfect the weight of her breasts would feel in his hands....

Trying to ignore the way his body had tightened and hoping the other occupants of the room didn't notice, he offered Katie the remaining mug, but she only shook her head.

"Next time you need to talk, try picking up a phone."

"Why didn't you tell me that the police department refused to provide protection? That you were paying for it?"

"Police departments aren't in the business of providing personal protection, Katie. Even if they wanted to, they don't have the budgets or the manpower." Looking down at his mug, he regretted his bluntness. She couldn't help that she was the first woman he'd looked at since his wife's death.

Her mouth tightened. "Thanks. But I can pay my own bills."

"Yeah." He took a sip of coffee, and looking over the rim, liking the show of defiance, added, "Well, we both know this one wasn't yours to pay. It was mine."

After several seconds, she looked away from his steady gaze. Had she realized what he was thinking? That somewhere mixed up in everything else they'd talked about these past three night, he'd found something he hadn't expected to. A connection to her.

He was aware of Martinez watching them both. "If you're worried about the arrangements, Katie, you needn't be."

"I'm not worried. I'm just tired of being consulted after they're made. It's my life."

He should have seen this coming. He'd sensed her frustration with the lack of progress. He knew he shouldn't be irritated with his brother for providing her with a computer, but he was.

Alec looked at Martinez, who still stood just inside the front door. "Maybe you should let Jack know what's happened. The phone's in the kitchen." His gaze returned to Katie. "And why don't we go into the other room?"

He showed her into his home office-den, the only room in the house he'd bothered to furnish fully. Some would say he'd traveled light when he'd left Philadelphia. Of course, some would have said he wasn't traveling at all, but running.

She didn't take the seat on the couch that he'd offered,

instead crossed to the windows where she pulled back the heavy green drapes to look out.

He sat on the edge of his desk and, putting the mug down next to him, waited for her to speak. Listening was always the key. Even during an interrogation, listening to what was said, to what wasn't being said, was the quickest path to answers.

They'd spoken on the phone nightly, but he hadn't seen her in four days. She looked tired, he decided. The early morning sun revealed what the dim foyer hadn't—the ravages of days on end filled with fear. The overload of adrenaline had left its mark in her restless movements, the fingers and eyes that never stopped moving, the tensing of shoulders and thighs and buttocks at the smallest of sounds. Battle ready, but too exhausted to be effective.

He obviously didn't like seeing her that way, but knew nothing he said or did would be able to alter her emotional state. He moved around the desk and sat in the chair.

"I didn't do a damn thing wrong, but I'm in prison." She turned to him suddenly. "I seem to have fewer rights than a convicted felon. At least inmates get a few hours outside each day. Weekly visitations."

"It's not forever, and that's the only way your safety can be guaranteed."

Maybe if he gave her a few details about the arrangements, the reasons behind them, she'd start to feel more in control.

"The man I've hired to protect you will be here tonight. He's good, really good. Comes from a Secret Service background and has been working in the private sector for the past five years. You'll both stay at Martinez's for a few days. Until I find another place and have a security system installed."

"How long is my sentence, Alec?" She walked toward him, her arms crossed again. "How many days or weeks or months?"

"As many as it takes."

"As many as it takes?" She offered a tight smile as she stopped in front of the desk. "That's a glib answer, don't you think?"

She placed her hands on the desk, her eyes bright, not with fear but with anger. "Not once has anyone asked me what I want. I came busting in here this morning because I was tired of being excluded from the decision-making process. And yet you still don't ask." Her expression hardened even further. "You could at least go through the motions."

"And what would that accomplish?" He rubbed the back of his neck. "There are no real choices to make. I wish there were."

"That's bullshit!"

"Is it?" His frustration level was climbing. Maybe he should try a different tack. "Is there something about the arrangements that you would like to see changed?"

Her mouth flattened. "One or two."

"Okay. Lets see if we can correct them, then."

"For starters, I want to move in here. And I want you to be the one to protect me."

What in the hell was she thinking? He set the cup he'd just picked up back down as he spoke. "That won't work. It's not safe."

"Nowhere is safe. That's what you said the other night. No matter where I go he will follow me."

"You have to give us more time to catch him. The DNA results aren't even in."

"How many months has it been since Jill died?"

The question took him by surprise, but he answered.

"Eleven months and four days." He could have told her the hours and the minutes, too, but didn't.

"I've checked the national averages. After one year, there's a seven percent chance Jill's killer," she said and then pointed at her chest, "my attacker, will be apprehended. Seven percent," she repeated. "The longer a murder goes unsolved, the less likely the killer will be caught."

"Each time a perpetrator acts, he increases his risk of apprehension." He let out a harsh sigh. "These things take time."

"Time? My mother's in a hospital in Arizona, Alec."

"I'm sorry. How serious is it?" He came out from behind the desk and tried to touch her, to offer some form of solace, but she held up her hand to ward off his comfort.

"They expect her to be fine. But the real point is that I can't go out there. What if you're right? What if he follows me? I'd be leading a killer to my parents' doorstep. I need an end to all this! To what's happening to me right now! I don't want to sit locked up in a house for months, hoping that a man who has remained invisible for nearly a year is suddenly captured. And I don't want to spend the rest of my life on the run, or even just looking over my shoulder, wondering if he's out there watching me. If I hear a noise in the night, I want to be able to believe that it's nothing to worry about."

He started to speak, but she cut him off. "When I left Miami, I told myself that I needed a change, that I was tired of living in a large city. That new scenery would help me grow as an artist. That I wasn't running. But I was. I allowed myself to become a victim. But not anymore."

She closed the distance between them. "Use me, Alec. Let's get this monster and make him pay for what he did to Jill, for what he nearly did to me."

"You have no idea what you're suggesting." He turned

away, but immediately turned back, and for the first time since they'd met, raised his voice. "No! I will not put you in danger!"

Straightening her already erect posture, she shoved the hair away from her temple. With carefully applied makeup concealing the bruising, the only undisguised remnants of the assault were in her haunted eyes and in the deep shadows beneath them.

"Okay." She started to back toward the door. "If you won't do it…"

He came after her, grabbed her before she made it to the door.

"What in the hell do you think you're going to do?"

"I'm going to get my life back! With or without your help!"

Chapter Six

Fifteen minutes later, Katie stood at the bottom of the ornate staircase, hugging a freshly brewed mug of coffee in her unsteady fingers. Alec had said he was going up to shower and change, to retrieve whatever it was that he wanted her to see before she made her final decision. But she now heard him on an upstairs phone. Was he canceling the bodyguard?

She hadn't left him much choice, had she? Even when she'd announced the ultimatum, she'd been worried that she wouldn't have the guts to see it through without him. Now she wouldn't have to find out.

She hadn't been playing fair. He held himself responsible for making her a killer's target, and because he did, he'd do anything to protect her. But he had no way to force her to go along with his plans for keeping her safe. He couldn't force her to do anything, but she could force his hand. Which was what she had done—forced him into a line of action that she knew he didn't agree with. And even though she was comfortable with her decision, she couldn't help but wonder about the wisdom of it.

She glanced at her watch. Just before eight. It was still too early to call her father. She'd wait a few hours before checking on her mother's condition. Her father hadn't really understood when she'd said she couldn't come right now, that perhaps in a few days she might be able to. She didn't like it that she couldn't be truthful with him about what was going on in her life. Liked it even less that he had to cope alone.

Feeling almost deflated after the confrontation with Alec, she scanned the foyer. Two chairs flanked the long chest along one wall. All looked to be expensive antiques. The rug underfoot showed wear, but also looked high-end.

Obviously, consulting work paid very well. She wondered why anyone would buy a house like this, though, and not bother to furnish the rest of it. Or why a widower would buy a place this size, at all. The absence of close neighbors maybe, she decided. And as far as the lack of furniture, maybe the consulting and Jill's investigation kept him too busy.

Unable to remain in one place too long, Katie prowled toward the large unfurnished room just to the right of the stairs.

Though she knew they must be original to the house, the heart pine floors looked nearly new. Whoever had built the home must have used pine underfoot as a cost-saving measure because the rest of the woodwork—the high, coffered ceiling, the rich paneling, the intricate moldings of the fire surround—was done in the Victorian era's more fashionable oak and was quite beautiful.

Hearing someone behind her as she took her first steps into the room, she glanced over her shoulder, expecting to see Alec. But the doorway remained empty. And in those few seconds, the silence grew heavier, like wet earth closing over her.

"Alec?"

Nothing. She shuffled backward. The sound of her own footsteps seemed to chase her as they rattled near the ceiling.

Feeling foolish, she took a deep breath and let it out slowly. She was losing it. If her own footsteps had her prepared to run, how was she going to get through the coming hours and days?

The answer was Alec. She'd be safe with him. Safe here in this house with the fancy alarm system and tall wrought-iron fence.

Coming here this morning had been the right decision. She wanted her life back. The fact that she was nervous and afraid was to be expected. But it was nothing she couldn't control, was it?

Two sets of French doors allowed easy access to the deep, covered porch running along the front of the house. Stopping at the first, she looked out at the dense natural vegetation that surrounded the turn-of-the-century home. Some would undoubtedly call the location pleasantly private. But when you found yourself the target of a killer, she suspected that even the middle of a county courthouse would seem too isolated for comfort.

A glimmer of something in the palmettos—a mirror or metal—forced her to blink. In the next instant, she wondered if she'd imagined it.

"Having second thoughts?"

At the sudden sound of Alec's smooth, even-toned voice just behind her, she bobbled the mug, and would have dropped it if his fingers hadn't closed over hers, steady and firm and warm. Until that moment she hadn't realized just how frigid her own were. Or just how desperate she'd been for the touch of another human being.

She lifted her gaze, intending to thank him, intending to step away, but something in Alec's rich chocolate eyes—kindness, understanding—kept her rooted to the spot.

The hair just above the collar of his dress shirt was still damp, and his handsome face was drawn in a serious expression. After days of staring at his computer-generated image, she'd nearly forgotten what it was like to be in the same room with him. Some people looked pretty much the same in person as they did in photos. Alec didn't. Photography couldn't depict the restless energy of this man, the sense that he was always watchful and in control.

"This isn't a good idea, you know," he said, his gaze remaining on her face while his thumb rubbed the back of her knuckles, once, twice, before releasing his hold. He stepped away, the momentary window of his eyes once more shuttered.

"I know," she said quietly. A bad idea in so many ways, but it was the only one she had, the only one that made any kind of sense. The only one she'd be able to live with.

He moved to the closest French door, his back to her, the early morning sun stealing beneath the porch just far enough to reach him. She sensed a level of indecision in him. As if even though he'd agreed twenty minutes ago, he still considered turning her down. She'd called his bluff. Perhaps he now considered calling hers.

And if he did, what should her response be? Since she'd played the only high card in her hand?

He ran a hand roughly through his hair. The conservative slacks and shirt only accentuated his well-toned, well-muscled body and his lean hips.

He continued to concentrate on the landscape, his fingers fiddling with the manila folder he held. Was what he wanted her to see in the file?

Should she ask to see? Or wait for him to offer?

She decided on the latter. She'd already pushed enough for one morning. "I want to thank you." She lifted the mug to her lips, but too late realized it was empty. Feeling foolish, she studied the bottom of the cup for several seconds before looking around for a place to set it. The only available surface in the room was the deep mantel fifteen feet away. With no other choice, she held the cup loosely by the handle.

"Don't thank me yet." Alec turned toward her, the brighter light at his back making it difficult for her to read his expression, but she could sense the rigidity in his body. She glanced down, saw the way his thumb worried the edge of the file, and knew that his hesitation was due to whatever was in it. She'd never been much good at waiting.

"What's in the folder, Alec? What is it that you want to show me?"

He ignored the question. "Before we go any further, I need to lay down the ground rules."

"Okay."

"I call the shots. No second-guessing my decisions. Or disobeying my orders."

Her eyes were once more drawn to what he held. His fingers were no longer moving, but instead crushed the folder. "I understand."

"No," he said. "You may think you do, but you don't."

She lifted her chin, more to appear confident than because she really felt that way. "Maybe you should tell me what it is that you don't think I understand, then."

He advanced toward her. With each step, he tapped the folder against his thigh. Her gaze ricocheted from it to Alec's face and back again. What did it contain?

"Your moving in here is going to push him to the limit.

He'll become even more unpredictable, less rational in his thinking. Not a cornered animal, but a rabid, starving one desperate for the meal that will keep him alive."

Katie's fingers tightened on the mug handle. "If this is your idea of a pep talk—"

He cut her off. "And he'll do anything to get to you, to satisfy his need."

When she would have turned away, he wrapped his fingers around her upper arm. "And here's the good part, Katie. If he really wants to get to you, if he's willing to ante up the ultimate price, trade his life for yours, then I may not be able to stop him."

The brutally honest words jolted her. But in the next second, when she'd caught her breath, she wondered if he was trying to scare her into changing her mind. But when she looked into his eyes, she realized she was wrong. What worried him most, what he feared most was that he'd fail. That something would happen to her. That he wouldn't blame himself for one woman's death, but for two.

She reached up and covered his hand with her own. "You're not telling me anything that I haven't already told myself. So, if you're concerned that I'm not scared enough, that I might not follow your orders and do something foolish, you needn't be. I've thought my decision through. And let me assure you that I'm terrified, more terrified than I have ever been in my life. So don't patronize me."

"Patronize you?" She could feel the tension in him, and felt it rising inside her as he continued to hold her arm, his eyes filled with not just fear, but also something darker. Something that appeared to be anger, but wasn't.

When he released her, she crossed to the fireplace, using the empty mug as an excuse to escape.

Alec followed. "Decisions should only be made when

you are in possession of all the facts. Don't you agree?" He pulled what appeared to be a black-and-white photograph from the folder.

"As an artist, Katie, you may be able to appreciate the catchy saying we use at Quantico." His gaze never left her face as he slapped the black-and-white photo up on the mantel, propping it there as if it were an Ansel Adams displayed on a museum wall. "If you want to know an artist, study his art."

She felt her jaw go slack, felt the shock of what she was looking at punch the last of the oxygen from her lungs.

The picture showed a woman's body splayed atop bed sheets soaked in blood, her hands and feet bound to bedposts. Candles burned on the nightstand. Blood trailed down the wall behind the bed and had been used to write something, but the smeared letters were illegible.

She covered her mouth to stifle the soft, harsh cry that climbed her throat. Dear God. Not a woman's body, Katie reminded herself, but the body of Alec's wife. Jill Blade's body. Jill, who in life had taught third grade. Had breathed and dreamed. Had loved.

Katie wanted to close her eyes and block out the image, but didn't. Alec was testing her. Testing her resolve. She needed to stand rock steady, show him that she was strong and determined.

Lowering her hand, she tried to force oxygen in and out of her lungs.

Don't personalize the woman. Concentrate on the scene, on the photo. Like a cardiac surgeon in the operating room, she had to disassociate, needed to tighten her focus so that it included only the heart and not the body it beat within.

She managed a shallow breath. She sensed Alec watching her. *Just a photo, A horrible picture.* It couldn't hurt her. She had to convince him that she was tough enough for what lay ahead.

But how could Alec stand to look at it? Even if he'd made a career of studying such scenes, how could he look and remain coldly unmoved by this one? Dear God—how could anyone survive such heartbreak and horror—to live with this dreadful image every minute of every waking and sleeping hour of every day?

Alec's voice was low and carried a hint of apology. "The man is no common monster, Katie. He's what nightmares are made of."

He nudged her, forcing her to take a small sideways step, just enough that she realized a second picture now rested inches to the right of the first. And two more at equal intervals beyond that. She hadn't seen him place any of them.

"Know the artist." Alec repeated, and she heard in his voice just how hard this was for him. He wasn't unmoved by what was in these photos, but hardened by it. How many times had he pulled them out and propped them here? How many times had his nightmares taken him back to that room? To the night he'd found his wife?

What exactly did that do to a man? What had it done to this man?

In the second photo, additional lighting had been added, making the writing legible.

REmEmBEr.

Nausea crawled up her throat. She wanted to turn away, to run away, but couldn't.

She made herself look at the third. It was a tight-angled shot and showed a bloody box cutter. The instrument of torture. Of violent death.

Swallowing the bile that climbed her esophagus, she turned to the last of the photos, certain nothing could be any worse than what she'd already seen.

She was naive, though. He'd saved the best for last.

She started to shake. It was her bedroom. The box cutter waited on the nightstand where candles had been lit. She was to have died in that room.

It was to have been her torture chamber.

This time she couldn't breathe, the tightness in her chest making it impossible. What had made her think she could do this?

She couldn't do it. She wasn't that brave, that courageous. No one was.

Stumbling backward, she lost her balance.

Alec grabbed her by the elbows and kept her from going down in a heap.

"I'm sorry. But you need to know what could happen." Like an adult talking to a small child, he lowered his face so that he could look directly into hers, his mouth a grim line. "There's no cowardice in changing your mind, Katie."

The words were right there, ready to come out, when suddenly something inside her bit them back. Hadn't she sworn that she was done with running, and equally finished with being a victim? Perhaps if Alec could have promised her that it would end in two or three months, even a year, she would have been willing to go back into hiding. But he couldn't. It could be two weeks or twelve years. And she couldn't live with that type of uncertainty. Never knowing when or if she'd get her life back.

"It's your call, Katie. Nothing has changed. The plans still stand. I didn't cancel the bodyguard and my brother has a safe place for you to stay."

Compassion and pain filled his dark eyes, and for the

first time she envisioned what the past eleven months had been like for him. The fact that he hadn't cited the hours and minutes when she'd asked didn't mean he didn't know them. Didn't mean he didn't think of the rapidly approaching and morbid anniversary.

He wanted the man who had killed his wife, desperately wanted to see justice done, but was too honorable to use her—his best and maybe only hope of seeing that happen.

She managed to step back, and he let her go, perhaps sensing that she needed the distance.

"Katie?"

"You want the truth? Something I just now realized?" She bit her lower lip briefly as she searched for the right words. "That if you're exposed to anything—even terror— for a long enough time, it loses its power. It doesn't go away. It's still there, but you can somehow deal with it when the day before you couldn't."

She glanced down at the floor. She didn't know the woman in those pictures, but in some ways, they were going to be tied to one another for eternity. Deep down in both their souls, they knew what made a monster.

Katie tightened her arms around herself and looked up, meeting Alec's gaze. "I'm scared. But not enough to make me run. Not enough that I'll allow myself to be a victim ever again. I want my life back. Not the one this killer has handed me, but the one of my own making."

"Okay," he said. There was quiet acceptance in his tone, as well. As if he understood the path she'd chosen. Perhaps he knew it was the same one he would have chosen for himself if the situation was reversed. "But if at any point you decide you want out, you only have to say the words."

She nodded. That moment had already come, but there was no going back.

TWENTY MINUTES LATER, having washed her face, Katie hesitated in the kitchen doorway. The room was a gourmet's theater with dark cherry cabinets, black granite countertops and gleaming stainless steel appliances.

Alec stood at what looked to be a commercial stove. He'd rolled back the sleeves of his white shirt, and a rust-tone dish towel rested over one shoulder. It was an odd image. The tough ex-FBI man stirring eggs, the picture of domestic talent. Had he done most of the cooking for him and Jill, or had she been equally talented in the kitchen? For the first time Katie allowed herself to think about Jill Blade, not as a victim, but as a living, breathing person. What had she been like, the elementary school teacher? They'd been married for nearly six years. Had it been one of those rare, truly blissful marriages?

Katie had been engaged once, several years ago, to a young doctor she'd met at a charity art auction. The engagement had lasted for nearly a year before she and her fiancé had mutually called it off. They'd realized that they made better friends than lovers. She expected to get married someday. Having been raised in a loving family, she wanted the same. But up until the past two years, most of her energies had gone into establishing her career in the art world.

Katie suddenly realized she was being stared at by a large black cat sitting at Alec's feet. As she stepped inside the room, the cat got up and strolled across the flagstone floor.

Casting a glance over his shoulders and spotting her, Alec removed the towel to wipe his hands.

"Have a seat."

She noticed the two placemats on either side of the bar top, and she slid onto the closest leather stool. The cat rose up on its back legs and sniffed her almost as a dog would.

"Where are your manners, cat?" Using a foot to nudge

aside the animal, Alec placed the plate of scrambled eggs and toast in front of her, along with a second mug of coffee.

She stared at the eggs for several seconds. Her throat stiffened at the idea of food. "I'm not hungry." She pushed the plate away as he sat opposite.

He shifted it back in front of her. "Eat. You've lost weight."

She wondered how he could tell. The oversized rugby shirt and shorts weren't exactly form-fitting. And he'd rarely seen her in anything that showed off curves. She'd always left tight-fitting, low-cut and skimpy to her twin. From the time they'd exchanged cradles for toddler beds, Karen had seemed to need to be the center of attention. First her parents', later it had been attention from the opposite sex.

Katie, on the other hand, had preferred the background. Or maybe, realizing that she'd already been relegated there, she'd accepted it.

That had changed after her sister's death. She'd come out of her shell, gradually at first, but more so when she'd attended the Ringling School of Art and Design, and had discovered that she, too, could shine.

Alec reached across and placed the fork in her fingers. "Rule number one," he said in a low voice, "in any competition. Stay stronger than your opponent."

She silently dipped the fork into the eggs.

"And rule number two?" she asked after several bites.

"Be better prepared. Have a plan. And have a contingency one, too."

"And do you have both?" She tore a corner off a toast wedge. She preferred more butter, but didn't bother to add it. The toast stuck halfway down her throat, and she used orange juice to wash it free.

"I have one," Alec said. "I'm working on the other."

"Can you tell me something about it, then?"

Setting his empty juice glass down, he seemed to weigh the request.

"We start by creating the illusion that you're no longer afraid of him. You go back to work and back to painting."

Back to work? She took a hurried sip of coffee. She hadn't expected him to say that, and wasn't certain how she felt about the idea. But she assumed he wouldn't ask her to do it if he didn't think she'd be relatively safe. Besides, the deal had been that she wouldn't question his decisions, so it probably wasn't wise to do so with the very first one.

"We'll let it be known that we're now involved and that you've moved in here. Maybe even suggest that we've been seeing each other secretly since shortly after you came to town. That should keep his focus solely on you."

Katie curled her finger into the mug's handle. "And then what?"

"We wait for him to make his move."

She sank her teeth briefly into her lower lip. "You mean we wait for him to come after me." She'd told him to use her, and it appeared as if he'd taken her at her word.

Unable to sit still, she picked up the plates and carried them to the stainless steel sink. The expansive window above overlooked the backyard. The swath of lawn quickly gave way to the natural beauty of century-old oaks, draped with Spanish moss. Against the blue of the early sky, the moss resembled hanks of torn, decayed cloth.

Katie's fingers trembled, and she quickly set the plates in the sink. She'd picked Deep Water because of its wild, "old-Florida" beauty and the chance for solitude, for the slower pace it offered. But now, looking out at those branches, remembering her attack, she would have given anything for royal palms and a mobbed beach.

"What about the other waitresses? If I go back to work, won't there be some danger for them?" She turned the water on. Instead of drumming against the sink bottom as it would have in a cheaper model, the water was nearly silent as it hit the thick-gauged stainless steel sink.

"He won't go for you at the café."

"How can you be so certain?"

"Because I know him. I know how he thinks. More importantly, I know what he needs." He raked a hand through his hair and followed her to the sink with the mugs, setting them on the counter. "The ritual is just as important as the killing. He needs time and privacy. He won't go after you in public because there's too big a chance he won't have either. He'll wait until he can get to you in private."

She felt her pulse kick a little faster at the idea. "How private?"

His mouth tightened. "We'll need to provide him with opportunities. But not right away. We'll let him get comfortable. Let him regain the confidence he lost when his first attempt failed."

"Won't he know he's being set up?"

"Yes. But he believes he's better than anyone else is. He's smarter, faster, more determined. And he believes he can get by me."

She sponged off the plate.

"You really think it will work? That we'll be able to catch him?"

As usual, his eyes gave away nothing. But his fingers did when they reached out and touched her. They weren't quite steady as they closed over her crossed forearms. Was he worried? Not that his plan wouldn't work, but that it might work too well, but that in the end, he wouldn't be able to keep her safe?

She looked up at him, her gaze meeting his, and yet all she could seem to think about was his touch, about how much she needed someone to hold her.

She wanted to feel… It didn't matter what, so long as it wasn't fear. She glanced down to where his hand rested on her sleeve. What would his fingers feel like on her bare skin? She envisioned them stealing beneath her shirt to press warmly against chilled skin. Katie felt herself tremble. Realized just how screwed up she was. She could find the courage to face a monster, but she couldn't ask Alec to hold her.

"You're going to have to trust me on this, Katie."

His fingers tightened briefly before falling away. She missed the connection immediately.

Reaching around her, he turned off the water. As he started to move away, she placed her hand against his chest. And when she did, both of them went instantly still.

Tension radiated from his body. From her own, as well. Her breathing became shallower. She recalled his heart hammering beneath her palm the night he'd rescued her. How safe he had made her feel.

Raising her chin, she met Alec's gaze. Seeing the desire there, her pulse kicked a little harder, and her throat tightened. When she'd reached out for him, she'd intended to ask him to hold her. She'd thought the only thing she wanted from him was to feel safe.

But looking into his eyes, she felt anything but that.

Uncertain, Katie dropped her gaze to his throat. Smooth skin. The scent of his cologne reaching her. The open collar of his starched shirt left a triangle of skin exposed.

What would his chest be like? What would it feel like

to lay her hand over his heart without a shirt in the way? To feel smooth male flesh beneath her palm instead of starched cotton?

And then sanity suddenly returned and she realized what she was doing. That she had just overstepped some invisible boundary.

Letting her hand drop, she backed away. It took her another second to look at him again.

"I trust you, Alec," she managed, but was surprised just how unsteady her voice was when she said it.

THIRTY MINUTES LATER, Alec sat at his desk. Martinez had delivered Katie's things and Alec had shown her to the guest room, suggesting she lie down for an hour or so.

He needed some time to get himself back on track, too. She'd taken him by surprise in the kitchen. But the way he'd become aroused when she'd touched him had been even more surprising. He couldn't allow her to distract him. No matter how desirable he found her. He needed to stay focused on keeping her safe.

He picked up two of the photographs he'd forced her to view. He couldn't forget the look on her face as she'd stared at each of them. He hadn't wanted to put her through any of it, but she needed to fully understand the magnitude of her decision.

And a picture had been worth a thousand words.

He looked at the photo, at the empty bed and unblemished white sheet, bisected by a trail of rose petals. Then turned his attention to the other black-and-white. Instantly his memory supplied the scent of fresh blood, and just beneath the heavy richness of it was the darker one of fear.

The olfactory sense was more firmly attached to memory than any other and he found himself suddenly back there, feeling the rage and pain and loss all over again. He'd often had to deliver bad news to a family about their loved one, had looked into the bleak eyes of those who had lost someone dear to them—a child, a wife—and allowed himself to believe that he understood what they felt. But he hadn't.

He compared the two photos. The most obvious difference was the lack of blood and a victim in one.

No. Katie was still very much a victim. An unbelievably brave one. She'd fought back that night, and she was still doing it. Not many woman had that kind of courage.

But Jill had also fought her killer. There had been signs everywhere that she hadn't gone quietly to her death. He'd never thought of her as a fighter. Kind and thoughtful, almost meek in some ways, but never physical. Even in their lovemaking, she'd been gentle and tentative.

And then the autopsy report had come back, and he'd understood her tenacity. She hadn't been fighting just for her own survival, but to save the baby. Their baby. The one she'd been desperate for and the one he hadn't even known about.

The last time he'd phoned, she'd hinted that she had a surprise for him, but he'd been distracted with his case and hadn't allowed himself to be drawn in by her excitement. Even now, that pained him. He'd been a good provider, but he hadn't been a good husband.

Alec laid the photos side by side on the desk, determined to stay focused on the present. There was something about the photo of Katie's bedroom… He could feel it tearing at the back of his brain, but he couldn't seem to force it to gel.

It would come to him. It always did. And in the meantime, he needed to nail down his plans for keeping her safe.

He glanced up when he realized Katie stood in the doorway. "Couldn't sleep?"

"I never can in the middle of the day." She advanced into the room. She had changed into cream slacks and a pale blue sweater, and anchored her hair back into one of those sensible styles women thought made them look sophisticated and pulled together. He preferred her hair down, but didn't have any right to voice an opinion. Nor did he have any right to be admiring the way the soft blue knit flowed across her breasts, or the way the beige slacks molded to her firm backside.

Which set of lingerie did she wear? He'd felt uncomfortable picking out bras and panties for a woman he didn't know very well and had turned the job over to a young clerk, returning only to pick them up on his way out of the mall.

It wasn't until he'd taken them from the store bag that he realized he should have told her the items were for his sister. They had felt cool and delicate in his hand, and had fueled thoughts that were neither.

He watched as she wandered over to the bookshelves and seemed to be scanning the titles. When she spoke, she still had her back to him. "Thanks again for buying the clothes. If you let me know how much I owe you, I'll write a check."

"Forget it." He placed the photos in the top drawer.

She still had her back to him. "So you were a profiler with the FBI for nine years?"

"No. Only for the last three. I worked in the Philadelphia field office for my first six years with the Bureau. Then I was recruited to work in the profile unit."

"So some astute higher-up recognized your gift?"

"I wouldn't call it exactly a 'gift.'" Some people tended to think profilers were one short step away from psychics, which couldn't be further from the truth.

"What would you call it, then? Magic?"

"Hardly. The media tends to glorify what profilers do."

He pushed back from the desk. "I don't do anything more than what you do countless times each day. I just do it with more awareness. Each time I visit a scene or look at a photo of one, or listen to a law enforcement officer describe what he's witnessed, I bring my experiences and knowledge into the equation, just as you do each time you get behind the wheel of a car—"

"I don't drive."

"But you have a license." He knew because he'd done a background check on her three days ago. And knowing what he did, he could guess at the reason she didn't drive. Her sister's life had ended behind the wheel, the driver of the other car involved in the accident charged with vehicular homicide.

"I didn't say I couldn't drive, I just don't." She didn't want to tell him. How far would she go not to talk about the accident?

"Why not?" Maybe that's why she intrigued him so much. She was mentally and emotionally complex. Everything looked neat and precise on the surface, but there were currents swirling just beneath.

"Because I don't. I keep the license updated so that I have a valid picture ID."

He realized that no matter what she had said in the kitchen earlier, she didn't trust him. He'd have to work on that, because at some point it would become important that she did.

"Profiling," he said, getting back to the original topic, having learned what he needed to know about her for the moment. "Profiling is nothing more than taking what you know and applying it to a situation."

"Any situation?"

"Pretty much." He walked from behind the desk. Katie

immediately turned her back to him. Evasion. He wondered if she realized in that simple action, she'd given herself away.

Allowing her the space she'd asked for, he moved to the window. "Let's say you're standing on a curb and see a car traveling down the street. The light turns red. The crossing signal flashes it's safe to walk, but you don't step off that curb until the driver slows, or you make eye contact. Seems like common sense, doesn't it? But what you have really done is profile the situation. You've taken the information you have—it's dangerous to step out in front of a moving car, occasionally drivers run red lights because they're in a hurry or not paying attention—and applied it to the situation. Only when the driver makes the appropriate response by slowing or making eye contact do you cross. Experience has said it's now safe to walk in front of the car."

"I suspect it's more involved than that."

"A bit."

He watched and waited as she picked a book out of the shelf, seemed to study it, going so far as to open the front cover—another way of distancing herself.

"He wrote the word *remember* on the wall. Why?" She still didn't look up.

"He wants me to remember something."

"But not what he did to… What he did that night?"

"No. That's just a bonus for him." It would have been more comfortable not to force his gaze to remain on her. "I believe he's somehow connected to one of my cases. That he feels I wronged him in some manner and is attempting to even the score. I'm not exactly popular with the prison population. In fact you'll find my picture above a number of toilets on death row."

"And he sends you a postcard each month." It wasn't a question.

"The first one was handwritten in Jill's blood. The rest have been typed."

Katie replaced the book. She kept her arms crossed as she stopped in front of him. "I'm sorry about your wife," she said quietly. "I should have said so sooner."

He hadn't heard those words in months and they affected him more than he would have expected. He was the one who turned away this time. Maybe it wasn't the words so much as the woman who had spoken them.

"Are you up for a drive?" he asked, and moved toward her.

"Where to?" She turned away again, this time he could have almost predicted her reaction to the request. "Look, Katie, if I ask you to do anything you're not comfortable with, you tell me. And asking questions is okay, too."

Facing him again, she waited.

"The café for starters," Alec said. He saw the look of uncertainty come over her face. No matter how hard she was trying to appear confident about what lay ahead, about his ability to protect her, she wasn't.

"Why there?"

He saw her take a slightly deeper breath as soon as she said the words.

"Because, if we're trying to convince him that we're intimate, it's going to be more believable if we show up in public looking as if we are."

She nodded. "I just didn't expect…"

Even though he had a fairly good idea what she wanted to say, he waited for her to go on.

"I just…" She broke off again. "I… It's going to be hard for me to face everyone there. They know what happened. They'll ask questions that I'm not sure I'll be able to handle." She looked at him directly. "I always do better coping when I don't have to talk about things."

Didn't they all, he thought. "I suspect that most of your coworkers will understand that you don't want to talk about what happened."

She closed her eyes briefly, but not before he saw the cornered look there. Again, he didn't let her off easy, waited for her to put into words what she was feeling. As he stood there watching her, Alec realized that they weren't so different—they both tended to hide behind carefully erected facades.

"But they'll still be looking at me, wondering…"

"I know it will be hard. But I'll be there with you. And I'll help as much as I can."

She was worried about that, too, he realized. So was he, though. Pretending to be intimate was always tricky, the touching appearing a bit too intentional. Even the conversation was difficult to pull off. If they were overheard, if someone really watched them… Perhaps he was pushing things too fast.

And perhaps he shouldn't have stopped the moment in the kitchen; maybe he should have allowed her to take it a bit further. And possibly he would have if he'd been certain that he wouldn't be tempted to take it even further still. He was going to have to be careful around her. She had a knack for continually reminding him that he not only had spent the past year looking for a killer, he had also spent it without female companionship.

Alec reached out and touched her shoulder. "If you're looking at me, they won't be thinking about what happened that night, they'll be wondering about what's going on between us. What will happen between us tonight."

Even as he said it, he realized those weren't the words

she needed to hear. "I'm sorry," he offered and allowed his hand to drop. "Usually I'm not quite this clumsy."

She nodded and stepped away. "Just let me a grab a jacket."

As he watched her go, he wondered. If she was having trouble stepping foot inside the café and confronting her coworkers, how was she going to handle their second stop this afternoon?

Chapter Seven

"I guess that's it, then," Katie said as they left through the Alligator Café's back door.

It was just past one in the afternoon. In the past thirty-five minutes, while they'd been inside, the temperature had dropped by at least ten degrees and cloud cover had moved in ahead of a predicted cold front.

Wrapping his hand around Katie's upper arm, Alec scanned the alley as they walked toward his SUV. Businesses on two parallel streets used the paved area for deliveries and employee parking. There had been fourteen cars when they arrived, but only twelve of those original vehicles remained. A small silver Buick and a beat-up green Ford truck were both missing, and the only new addition was a yellow Mercedes that belonged to the owner of the antique shop across the way.

A sharp breeze gusted, pushing an empty plastic bag toward them, but he ignored the movement, focusing instead on the Dumpster just ahead.

They'd stayed at the restaurant only long enough to drink a cup of coffee and for Katie to get her work schedule for the rest of the week. He'd planned to linger, perhaps ordering lunch, but had realized shortly after they'd sat down that they were going to need to work on the couple thing. With any luck, this time at least, anyone who had observed them would take her stiffness to mean that she was angry with him.

Still ten feet from the car, Alec used the remote to unlock the black Explorer, again scanning the length of the alley for movement. He opened the door at the same time he released his hold on Katie.

She stepped around the door, but instead of sliding in, she met Alec's gaze. The breeze tugged her dark hair forward so that it sifted across her cheek and along the line of her jaw, the ends playing at the corner of her full lips. He'd been watching her mouth more and more, and even now wondered what it would feel like beneath his own.

She scraped the hair away. "Do you think we fooled any of them in there?"

"No. I think we're going to need to work on it a bit more. At least the touching in public part."

The wind shoved her hair across her cheek again, and Alec reached out, intending to push it back. He saw in her eyes the moment she realized his intent. Her own hand shot up before his fingers could make contact. Instead of withdrawing his hand, Alec let it settle over hers.

"You're going to have to get accustomed to my touching you, Katie." And he was going to have to learn how to control what he felt each time he got near her. "You're not much of an actress." Her fingers trembled beneath his.

Her lips were softly parted, and, as he watched, her tongue moistened the bottom one. He could feel the tension in her, tension similar to what they'd both experienced in the kitchen this morning.

He closed the distance between their bodies, his other hand coming up to frame her face. Her eyes were dark

and deep, the kind of eyes that could suck even an unwilling man into their depths. He may not have been an
unwilling man, but he was a cautious man. Far safer to
take this next step where there was no possibility of it
going any farther.

Alec lowered his mouth toward hers. "I think we need
to get this behind us," he said just before his lips settled
over hers. He felt her go still, and perhaps he would have
drawn back, but several of Katie's coworkers had exited
the back door and watched them. He deepened the kiss,
and after several seconds she relaxed, her lips opening
beneath his, her fingers fisting into his shirt.

How long would it take before she noticed that, while
he could control many things, he was still a man?

She suddenly stiffened. When she ducked her chin to
end the kiss he let her go and stepped back. His own
breathing was uneven, and he suspected his eyes would
reveal pretty much what hers did at that moment—sexual
hunger.

"That should dispel any notions your coworkers might
have about our relationship."

Katie glanced over his shoulder just in time to see the
rear door of the café close. She looked back at him, her lips
void of their usual pink gloss, her eyes still dilated. "Yes."
She offered a tight smile just before she turned away.

KATIE WATCHED out the side window for several minutes
after they pulled onto Alligator Creek Road.

She could still taste Alec, could still feel his warm,
male lips moving on hers. At the memory of his tongue
sweeping the inside of her mouth, she felt a wave of
desire build low in her body, similar to what she'd felt this
morning in the kitchen.

It was just sex, though. Her hormones kicking up their heels. Though she'd contemplated the possibility before the attack, she had no intention of getting involved with Alec now. And she suspected Alec felt pretty much the same way. They shared a very important common goal, and allowing anything to get in the way of that goal would be foolish. Especially something as fleeting as physical desire.

But that didn't change the way the kiss had affected her. The way the man affected her.

"Perhaps I should apologize for the way I handled that back there," Alec said.

"So that's not standard operating procedure for the Bureau?"

He took his eyes off the road long enough to glance across at her. "Not when working with a victim."

The word hung there between them. Maybe he'd used it because he knew how it would affect her. Or to remind her of the real reason he'd just kissed her—to convince a killer to come after her.

"No apology required," Katie said and glanced out the window. The honest truth was she didn't know if she was ever going to be at ease around Alec. Even now, there was a low hum of awareness that seemed to arc between them. At least for her. Other than the kiss, he seemed to be completely comfortable around her.

Katie rested her head back and closed her eyes.

Not too many moments later, the Explorer's tires vibrated across railroad tracks.

Katie's eyes shot open, and seeing the canopy of ancient oaks sweep across the moon roof, the pit of her stomach dropped like a basketball through a hoop.

She straightened. "Where are we going?" But she already knew.

Alec glanced at her. "Your place. To pack up photo albums and anything else that you want out of there. Maybe some of your art things, too."

He turned into Hibiscus Park, the SUV moving slowly past homes where the vibrant green of well-tended lawns was heightened by flower borders of bright pinks and reds and whites, where the late-model cars of retirees were kept showroom clean and the minivans of harried young mothers weren't.

The knot in her stomach expanded up into her chest. Her breathing quickened.

She turned in the leather seat until she faced Alec. "I don't think I can go in there." She heard the slight hitch in her voice. It wasn't just the room that terrified her; it was the image of the faceless man standing next to the bed.

"Listen, Katie," Alec said and there was a calm quality to his voice. "Not many women would have done what you did this morning. Especially not after seeing the photos. You're a strong lady. Maybe what's happening now is just the first time you've been tested, so you aren't aware of how strong."

He covered her clasped hands with his own. "Take it easy. If you don't want to go in, I'll go in and get the things for you. You can wait in the car."

"Thanks." She'd expected to feel relieved, but didn't. It had been only several hours since she'd assured him she could handle whatever catching this monster would entail, but here she was already refusing a simple request to walk into an unoccupied house.

As Alec pulled to the curb and turned off the engine, Katie glanced at the bungalow she'd called home for just over two months. It appeared to be pretty much like the others in the neighborhood, only a bit more down in the heel. The lawn obviously hadn't been cut since she'd last done it, and almost as if in victory, weeds waved above the thinning turf. It might look a little sad, but it certainly didn't look like a house of horrors.

It would take only a matter of minutes to grab the albums and her journal. The art supplies would take only a few more, and she needed something to distract her. Less than five minutes. Three hundred seconds. She could handle anything for that long, couldn't she?

When he reached for his door handle, she did the same.

"Are you sure?" Alec asked.

"Yeah." She was sure she wanted to do it. She just wasn't sure how she was going to act once she got in there.

As Alec retrieved the flattened boxes and the roll of packing tape he'd brought from the back of the SUV, she waited next to the truck. Her neighbor two doors away, a widower of many years, lifted a hand in a wave. Some of the tightness in her chest eased as she was forced to return the smile and wave.

Alec led the way up the walk. When the front door was pushed open, the house exhaled a dank breath of air.

"A cleaning crew came through yesterday, so most of the dusting powder has been taken care of, and they straightened up what they could, but there will be lots of things out of place."

After flipping on the foyer light, he scanned the interior before turning back to her. As he did, his jacket fell open enough to reveal his weapon. She'd never been fond of guns. Until now.

Having waited outside until the last minute, she now stepped in. He shut the door behind them and locked it, even going so far as to put the chain on. "Wait here while I have a quick look around and turn on some lights for us."

The house carried a sharp chill that seemed to penetrate bone deep. She rubbed her upper arms. Obviously, her landlord had shut off the heat.

Turning, she saw the damaged plaster just outside the opening to the dining room. Inside her head, she could hear the explosion of those shots. She'd been fighting to get her feet back on the ground as he dragged her backward, her fingers clawing at the forearm crushing her windpipe, then at the arm with the gun.

She forced herself to look away. She'd be much better off if she didn't think about that night. Though Alec had done a cursory inspection of the living room before moving on to the others, he returned to open the drapes and turn on the two lamps.

Katie hadn't moved from where he'd left her. "You could have picked up the albums and even some of my art supplies any time over the past few days. You didn't need me."

"You're right," he said.

"So that's not really the reason you brought me here, is it?"

"No. It's not."

"Then what is?"

Alec grabbed her hand. "There are two places in this town where he will expect you to turn up first. Where you work and where you used to sleep."

The panic she'd been keeping corralled threatened to break loose again. She took a deep breath, almost wishing she hadn't asked.

"And," Alec added, "the main reason I brought you here was that to get beyond what happened to you is going to require work from you, and that work has to start here where it happened. With your seeing this house for what it is. Just a house."

Katie unconsciously lifted her right hand to cover the fading bruises on her throat. All she wanted to do was get back to Alec's house, one of the few places she felt safe. As long as he was at her side.

"Do you think we could get this over with, then?" she asked.

He gave her a smile that she suspected was meant to encourage. "Sure."

Walking slowly toward the kitchen, she trailed her fingers along the foyer wall and allowed Alec's words to roll repeatedly through her mind. *It's just a house. Just a house. A house.*

Houses didn't have souls that could be tainted with the deeds that happened within them. Whatever she was feeling right now—the heavy ugliness of violence—was a manifestation of her own emotions and imagination.

The door at the end—her bedroom door—had drifted partially closed, as it always did. Where had *he* been that night? In the darkened dining room? In her bedroom? Maybe he'd expected her to head there to change—her usual path when she came home at night—and when she hadn't, he'd grown impatient. She realized he must have been watching her before that night, in order to know where she lived, her schedule.

She stopped at the kitchen opening. The mess on the floor was gone. Chairs had been neatly pushed in around the breakfast table. One sat at an odd angle, the bottom portion of a leg missing. She could kiss her security deposit goodbye.

She could feel Alec right behind her, not intruding, letting her set the pace, but close enough should she need him. She was determined not to.

She stopped outside the bedroom door, but couldn't make herself nudge it open. Just as she hadn't been able to walk those twenty feet down the empty aisle between the funeral home chairs to her sister's casket.

"Its okay, Katie. Everything from that night has been removed."

Her fingers remained curled until they reached the glass knob. She had regretted not making that trip, regretted not touching her twin one last time. And, just as that regret haunted her, the memory of this room would if she didn't face it.

The door swung inward when she pushed it, stirring the stale air. An unfamiliar scent lingered, perhaps that of the fingerprinting powder, but just beneath that was the smell of her perfume. And maybe of the candles, too. But the soft glow of the bedside lamp revealed a benign room. Lavender sheets, a set that had been in the top of her closet, covered the bed.

The wall area above the bed was still blank, the picture that had hung there missing. The police probably had it. She recalled the photo she'd seen this morning, the word scrawled in blood above another bed.

God. She'd been so lucky. Just as she had the night her sister Karen died. Death had been so close, and she had escaped.

Only she hadn't felt lucky then, and she wasn't now.

She allowed her glance to take in the rest of the room. The cheap pickled-oak furniture, the small bookcase behind the door. The painting just above the bookcase—a young boy paddling out on his surfboard, his father on a second board paddling alongside. She'd titled the piece *A Long Boarder's Right of Passage*. She'd hung it there so that it was the first thing she saw every morning. It had reminded her of the water she missed, and of the summer she and Karen had learned to surf.

Alec had moved to the center of the room. The faint shadow of a late-afternoon beard and the dark intensity of his gaze as he watched her now, made her aware of just how much her impression of him had changed in the past four days. Before that night, she'd seen him only as a very attractive man, one capable of making her pulse quicken with a simple look. More recently, she'd seen him as the only one capable of righting her world. She now realized he could easily be both.

"Would it be better if I got out of the way while you packed?"

"No…umm…no." Her facial muscles refused to cooperate when she tried to smile. "Please stay. It's not going to take long."

Katie knelt in front of the small bookshelf. Where her arrangement of the books had been haphazard, they were now placed in ascending height from right to left. Art volumes filled the top shelf, novels the second and family photo albums the third.

After putting together and placing one of the boxes near the bookcase, Alec moved to the window.

She pulled the half a dozen photo albums from the bottom shelf and placed them on the floor. Dusting powder clung to the outside covers.

She flipped open the top album and saw that the same dust had sifted between the photos and their plastic sleeves.

If the police had gone to the trouble of checking the inside pages, did that mean they thought he'd sat here in her bedroom going through the albums? Had his fingers brushed across the faces of her sister and her parents, of her close friends? Her fingers shook as she slammed closed the cover. God, she hated this!

She looked up, hoping Alec hadn't noticed. But he had.

Something in his eyes gave him away. He knew exactly what was going on in her head. What she was thinking.

"You really are very talented," he commented. He'd wandered from the window to stand in front of the painting of the two surfers.

"Don't look so surprised." She managed a weak smile.

"I'm not." He glanced down at her. "I just hadn't realized you did anything but landscapes."

She knew he'd been in the house several times over the past four days, so there was little chance that he hadn't seen the painting. He was just trying to help her cope by distracting her. There were many layers to Alec. The rough professional who gave orders and expected them to be followed, the polite stranger, and then this man, observant and even kind.

She placed the album in the box beside her. "I hear that your brother's a surfer. What about you?"

Alec retreated to the window again. The action didn't surprise her. She'd already caught on to the fact that he didn't like to talk about himself.

He parted the blinds to look out. "I taught him."

"You?" He didn't seem the surfer type.

He glanced over his shoulder. "Don't look so surprised."

She smiled at that. "I'm not." She tried wiping some of the black powder off her hands using a piece of paper she found on the shelf, and then noticed that some of it clung to her jacket sleeve. "Well, maybe I am a little bit. I can't picture you as a beach bum."

"But you can picture Jack as one?"

"Yeah." She narrowed her eyes as she looked up at him again. "I think it's his blond hair and the tan. And I sense this irreverent streak in him."

"That's Jack."

She climbed to her feet, one of the albums still in her hand. "Were you close growing up?"

"No. There are six years between us, which isn't much when you're adults, but it was when we were kids. Most of the time I just considered him a nuisance." He moved away from the window. "My folks took a place at the beach for two months one summer. He'd just turned twelve, and I hadn't quite made it to eighteen."

"Was that when you taught him to surf?"

"Yeah. My mother was against it. Too many sharks and rip currents."

He chuckled, his whole face seeming to relax at the memory. In that brief moment, she saw what he must have been like that summer. Deep tan, hair longer than it was now and a quick smile. And the eyes… There would have been hope there.

She dropped the album in the box with the other one.

"We'd leave early, saying we were meeting some friends for a game of volleyball, and be gone all day. I think Dad knew what was happening, but he was happy that Jack and I were connecting. He probably figured if we hadn't by the time I went off to college, we never would."

Katie moved to the dresser as Alec talked. Ignoring the clothes, she grabbed her journal from the bottom drawer. It, too, showed signs of having been dusted. The possibility that it had been read—by the killer, by Alec or some other officer of the law—left her feeling as if she'd been laid open on a coroner's slab.

She glanced over her shoulder, taking in the room, thinking just how close she had come to the morgue. It was the kind of image that really drove home her own mortality. Made her wonder if she had made the wrong decision after all.

Her fingers trembled. She took a deep breath. No. She wasn't going to cave in now. She'd made it this far, she could keep it together for another few minutes.

"Katie?" Alec stopped his wandering around the room. "Are you okay?"

She took another deep breath and let it out slowly. She just needed to keep her mind elsewhere. "What beach was it…that you went to that summer?"

Moving in behind her, he caught her gaze in the dresser mirror. She saw in his dark eyes that he understood what she wanted from him.

"New Smyrna," he said. "One morning we took off early and drove almost to Miami to get some good waves. A hurricane had passed just off shore and kicked up some bigger surf.

"Everything was fine. I'm sitting there waiting to catch a wave and I look over and see Jack's board being carried in, but no Jack. Two hundred miles from my parents, my brother has disappeared, and I don't know what to do. And then I feel something latch on to my leg. For half a second I think it's a shark and that it's already gotten Jack, and has come back for me."

He stepped back. "But it was just Jack. He'd been messing with the board's leash, actually had it off his ankle, when a wave took him broadside. The undertow caught him and dragged him out."

As she listened, she tried to picture the two men as boys, but found it difficult. "And you hadn't noticed any of that happening?" She dumped the contents of the jewelry box onto the dresser. Several loose shell beads from a broken anklet dribbled onto the floor. Ignoring them, she picked out the good pieces of jewelry.

"Notice? No. I was thinking about the blond coed who

had moved in next door. I was trying to figure out how I was going to separate her from her jock boyfriend."

"And did you?" Katie asked. She had no difficulty picturing him with some cute blond cheerleader. Was that his type?

"Yeah. Unfortunately, I did."

Katie looked up at the serious note in Alec's voice. "She was trouble?"

"No. It's just that once she came on the scene, Jack and I stopped catching waves together. I didn't realize a kid brother was more important than a long-legged blonde."

She sensed that he was uncomfortable with how much he'd revealed to her in that one story. Alec didn't let people get too close. She had assumed that he'd built the wall around himself after Jill's murder. But perhaps he'd been erecting the barrier long before that. Perhaps her death had only been the last brick sliding into place, finally cutting him off from those around him.

He turned back to her, all emotion once more locked away. "Are you done in here? If you are, maybe we can make a quick pass through your studio and grab some things."

She glanced around the room. Alec had been right in his assessment of both her and the house. It was just a house. In the morning, she'd call her landlord and tell him to give everything else to charity.

Her gaze landed on the painting of the two surfers. "Nearly done."

She lifted the painting down from the wall, studied it for several seconds. She'd never be able to look at it and not remember recent events.

She turned to Alec. "I want you to have this. To remind you of that summer."

Chapter Eight

It was still early, just after five in the afternoon when Katie piled the cardboard box she'd just emptied with the other two beneath the table in the small room that linked Alec's kitchen to the large solarium. With east-facing windows, the space had probably been used as a breakfast room at one time.

She'd chosen it for her studio because of its proximity to the kitchen and den, the two rooms that Alec obviously used, and because it was adjacent to the solarium.

She had even briefly considered setting her things up in the glassed-in space, but she hoped to do some painting at night and knew that all that glass would make her feel like a pork chop in a butcher's case.

As it was, she could cart her easel out there during the day and keep busy by painting one of the many palms or orchids that filled the space.

She stuck a handful of brushes, shafts first, into a mason jar. Alec's cat jumped up on the table and immediately hopped into the box she was unloading.

She smiled at the animal. "Comfortable?"

She looked up when Alec walked in with another box.

"This is the last of the art supplies." He placed it on the end of the table next to the one with the cat, and the cat immediately tried it on for size. As he peeked over the top, Katie ran a hand down his back. "What do you call him?"

"Since he's always underfoot, I've never had any reason to name him." He reached in, scooped the cat out of the box and placed it on the floor. "Did you want me to bring the boxes with the albums in here or put them upstairs?"

"Upstairs is fine."

He started to leave, then turned back. "If you need anything, just ask. I'll make us some dinner later, but for right now, I should make some preparations for tomorrow."

"Actually," she said before he reached the door, "there is something I need."

He turned back. "What's that?"

"To thank you. For everything. For this morning, for agreeing to let me stay here. And for this afternoon." She dropped the paint tubes she'd been sorting into the box. "You were right. I did need to go back to the house one more time."

His expression didn't change, but she thought she saw something briefly in his eyes, something she couldn't even begin to name.

"And I'm sorry about the kiss," he said.

Because she wasn't, she offered a tight smile, but nothing more. As he again turned to go, she pushed away from the table where she'd been leaning. "And I want you to know that I'll go the distance. I'm not a quitter."

He nodded, his face serious. "I'm not one, either."

ALEC PLACED the painting Katie had given him on the mantel where he'd propped the photos earlier, then stepped back. A small recessed light concealed in the twelve-foot ceiling brought the piece to life. The blue-green water appeared to be rising beneath the two surfers. Sunlight pierced the surface and revealed the dark ribbons of sea grass floating just beneath. Katie had studied at the Ringling School of Art and Design in Sarasota. It wasn't a cheap education. But Katie's parents, who had lost one child, wanted to give Katie the best.

Alec studied the face of the young boy. You could see the excitement in his eyes as he looked over at his father. It really was a remarkable painting.

It was the only piece of hers that had been hanging in the bungalow. And from what he could tell, the only piece she'd brought with her from Miami.

So why had she brought it?

In his experience, it was the *why* that was important.

Working the kind of cases he had during his career had left him fairly jaded. He was rarely shocked anymore by the things people did to one another or even to themselves. But their motives, their reasons for doing things, occasionally those could still surprise him.

He took an additional step back from the painting, but continued to study it. In a gallery, the piece would have brought more than three thousand. He knew its value because he'd seen appraisals for some of her other pieces on the Internet.

Her artistic ability was only one of her characteristics that intrigued him. Katie Carroll was a woman of subtle layers. She didn't actually deceive those around her, but she felt no compunction to dispel their notions about who she was. She didn't waitress because she needed a paycheck, and yet every one of her coworkers probably thought she did. Did she avoid telling them because she wanted to fit in—something she seemed to do with surprising ease—or was there another reason?

Katie Carroll was financially stable and was considered a rising star in the art world. On the surface, she seemed to have it all. Loving parents. An enviable bank account and status in her chosen profession. She was certainly attractive—something she tended to either ignore or play down. But even knowing all that, he didn't know what made her tick.

He would before it was all over.

"SOMETHING SMELLS DELICIOUS," Katie said several hours later when she stepped into the kitchen to find Alec at the stove.

After arranging her studio, she'd taken a stroll around the solarium, and had even sat for a few moments on one of a pair of fainting couches at the room's center. She tended to doubt that Alec had purchased the pieces when he had yet to furnish the large living room, so suspected the previous owner had left the antiques behind. Which seemed odd because they were so beautiful.

Alec looked up from whatever it was that he was stirring. A towel draped his shoulder again. He nodded at a glass of red wine on the end of the breakfast bar. "That's for you. Dinner will be ready in a few minutes."

"People who actually seem to enjoy cooking amaze me. Men especially." She wandered over to look in the pot. It appeared to be some type of soup.

"Seafood gumbo," he supplied as he dipped a spoon in to give it a stir.

She scanned the nearly spotless counters and the sink with its one rinsed dish. She'd always admired people who were neat and organized. Both seemed to be beyond her.

"When Dad retired, he briefly took up cooking. He went for the recipes requiring eighteen ingredients and a full-time assistant to keep ahead of the mess he created. I think that's one of the reasons Mom agreed to the motor coach. At least he'd be out of her kitchen."

"You don't cook?" Alec asked, turning down the heat.

"No. I majored in microwave and minored in the can opener."

He grinned, his eyes showing his surprise. "What do you usually eat, then?"

"Sandwiches and salads mostly. Occasionally, some takeout."

A laptop computer sat next to the wine. As she picked up the glass, she saw herself doing so on the screen.

"What's this?"

"I thought you might feel more comfortable if you saw firsthand how I'll be able to keep track of what's going on at the restaurant even when I'm not right there with you."

She picked up the glass, but didn't take a sip. Instead, she searched for the camera, using her image to guide her. She finally located it propped on top of a decorative wall plaque. Small, innocuous. She wondered where he intended to put it in the restaurant.

She took a sip of the wine. "Where will you be?"

"The library just down the street. If you need me, I can get to the restaurant in less than thirty seconds."

That was fast. But would it be fast enough should something happen?

She leaned against the opposite counter. "So what's the plan?" she asked. "What happens tomorrow? What should I expect?"

He dumped rice into a pan of water. "I'll take you in and have my usual breakfast. I'll place the camera then. Afterward, I'll leave."

She almost lost her grip on the wineglass, sloshing some of the liquid on her hand. "Anything else I should know?"

"You should try to stay in the main dining room as

much as possible. Don't allow yourself to be alone. And, if at all possible, try to relax."

The wine almost went down the wrong way with that one, but she managed to nod. "Relax? How would you suggest I accomplish that?"

"You'll do fine. The first hour or so will probably be tense. After that, it will start to get better. Just don't allow yourself to relax too much. Stay alert." He grabbed plates out of a cabinet and placed them on the counter. "Remember, I need thirty seconds. It's going to be up to you to make sure I have it."

Instead of giving her confidence, Alec's plans were making her more unsettled. Not because she didn't think they would work, that she'd be relatively safe—as safe as possible given the circumstances—but because it made tomorrow morning seem so much closer, and the danger so much more real. As with anything—it was one thing to talk about it and another to do it.

But this was what she wanted, right? She needed to stay firmly focused on that fact. If she wanted her life back, she needed to take it back. It was as simple as that.

Alec selected silverware out of the drawer. When he swung his attention back to her, he looked more concerned now than he had several moments earlier. "There's something else I need to mention to you. I had a phone call earlier." He dumped the rice into a bowl. "Carlos Bricker has dropped out of sight."

Katie finished the wine in one long gulp. So her ex-boyfriend, who had made a number of her paintings disappear three months ago, had now gone underground? Things just got better and better, didn't they?

She poured herself another glass from the bottle sitting on the counter. "How did you find that out?"

"I had a man keeping an eye on him, not a close one, but just to be certain he stayed in Miami."

"Why do that?"

"To be sure he didn't become a complication. It appears that he has."

"Just because he isn't in Miami?"

"No. Because it appears he knows where you are and might be heading this direction."

AT EIGHT the following morning, the breakfast rush at the Alligator Café was in full swing. Two of the waitresses, both college students, and the busboy had no-showed, leaving Katie, Betty and a third waitress waiting additional tables and bussing their own dirty dishes.

Katie pocketed the generous tip left by a couple of mechanics, and then loaded the heavy-duty plates, cups and silverware into a bin. Having spent most of the night staring up at the ceiling and listening to the floorboards creak, she was exhausted. If not for the overload of adrenaline in her system, she would have been flat on her face.

She knew her coworkers and even several of her regular customers had another theory about why there were dark circles beneath her eyes. Evidently, the kiss in the alley yesterday had done its job. She wasn't used to hearing her sex life discussed by people whose last names she didn't know. But as uncomfortable as it was, it was nothing compared to how much her feet were hurting her. She was giving some serious thought to going barefoot. Why in the heck hadn't she remembered to get her work shoes last night?

As she wiped the table clean, the usual sounds of silverware clattering against dishware, the ongoing throb of male conversations, punctuated by sharp laughter and occasional swearing, and the scent of eggs and bacon grease

and toast surrounded her as they had for two months now.
In the past, she'd rarely paid attention to the conversations
of her customers, but today she found herself listening to
talk of cattle and oranges and some upcoming political
rally.

She glanced often to where Alec sat near the back of the
restaurant. Either he wasn't suffering the adrenaline
overload, or his years with the FBI had taught him to cope.
In another fifteen or twenty minutes, he'd be leaving. She
still didn't know how she was going to handle that moment.

Hefting the load of dirty dishes onto a hip, she motioned
for the party of four men near the door to have a seat at the
table. She enjoyed most aspects of her job, clearing and
wiping down tables wasn't one of them.

As she headed for the kitchen with the dishes, the front
door opened again, the usual sharp *ding* going nearly
unheard by most of the room's occupants. Turning to see
who had come in, she felt the first jolt of fear hit her
midchest. The man was backlit, but she would know him
anywhere. Carlos. She backed away.

Her gaze swung to where Alec sat. As their gazes connected, he rose in what seemed like slow motion. His hand
reached inside his jacket as he started forward.

She looked back at the man. He stood still just inside
the door.

The heavy throb of blood in her ears muffled the surrounding chatter. Her breath came soft and shallow and too
fast.

Move!

Around her, no one seemed to notice. They continued
to go about their business, eating eggs, munching toast,
sipping coffee.

She took a step backward. She started to turn, but her

foot hooked a chair leg. The bin of dishes slipped off her hip and crashed to the floor.

Everyone looked up at the sound, including the man just inside the door. Their eyes connected for the briefest of moments, but it was long enough for her to realize her mistake.

She quickly knelt to pick up the broken dishes. It wasn't Carlos. The height, build and coloring were the same, but it wasn't her ex-boyfriend. And even if it had been, she was overreacting. She might not want to see him, but it wasn't Carlos who was trying to kill her.

A man sitting nearby scooped up several large pieces of broken plate from beneath his feet and placed them in the bin. "Are you okay, Miss?"

"I'm fine." She tried not to look at him. Her hands were shaking. In fact her whole body still trembled. "I can get this. Enjoy your breakfast."

Alec squatted next to her. "Are you okay?"

Embarrassed, she continued to pick up pieces of broken dinnerware. "I'm fine. I just lost my grip."

Alec's fingers wrapped around her wrist, stilling her action. Her pulse raced strong and erratic beneath the pressure. And it wasn't only because of what had just happened. Even in the crowded restaurant, there was something about the two of them being down there on the floor that created an odd sense of intimacy. And right then, that wasn't what she needed. She needed space and a few moments alone.

Alec's fingers brushed across her wrist. The bruises there were nearly a week old now, but had yet to fade completely.

"Fine, huh?" Alec asked.

Betty, the head waitress and sometimes cook, stooped to help. "You okay, hon?" Betty placed a mug in the bin, then used the dishrag to wipe up the worst of the food mess on the floor. "What happened?"

"I tripped." Katie stood, taking the bin with her. "You know me. Two left feet."

Betty reached for the dishes. "Let me have that. You go get yourself cleaned up."

Glancing down at the front of her, Katie realized she had eggs and coffee and orange juice splattered everywhere. "Thanks." When she turned, she came face-to-face with Alec again. She pushed past him, anxious to reach somewhere quiet, somewhere where she didn't feel as if everyone was watching her.

She headed for the storage room where she kept a change of clothes and her purse. The doctor had given her a whole bottle of Valium right after the attack, but determined to shake her fear, she'd refused to take even the first one. But not anymore. From here on out, she'd take any help she could get, including drugs.

She poured one into her sweaty palm. Just enough to take off the edge. Just enough to get her through the next few hours. She stared at the small pill, recalled how, following her sister's death, the doctor had given her mother the same prescription.

But Annie Carroll hadn't taken the first one.

Katie dropped the pill back into the bottle and shoved the container to the bottom of her purse. Not today. Today she could handle the fear.

The room was no more than ten by ten and the walls were completely covered in crude wood shelving filled with the usual restaurant supplies: the hefty cans of green beans, the large bags of flour and rice. Even after repeated washings, the bare concrete floor seemed impregnated with the mustiness of dirt.

In spite of the smell, she kicked off her shoes. She untied the apron and tossed it aside before ripping off the T-shirt with the large alligator on it. Just a few more hours. She just had to hang in there until after the lunch crowd. Bending, she used the discarded shirt to wipe most of the mess off her legs. She grabbed a clean one from the shelf above. She pulled it on over her head, shoving first one arm, then the other through. The shirt still caught above her breasts, she looked up.

Alec stood in the doorway, his expression revealing nothing of what he might be thinking. "The door was open."

How long had he been standing there? She tugged the T-shirt down over her scarred rib cage and tucked it into her waistband. Had he noticed them? The scars had faded quite a bit over the years, but she still felt self-conscious of them. "Anyone ever suggest you wear a bell around your neck?"

"Like a cat? No. There have been other suggestions, though." He offered up a smile. "Not nearly as polite."

She was being unfair. He'd just come to see if she was okay. "Sorry," she mumbled. "I guess I'm nervous."

"What happened out there?"

"The man who came in looked a lot like Carlos." She tied a fresh apron around her waist. "I keep this mantra going inside my head—you're okay, you'll survive this— but sometimes, between the blood pounding in my ears, my heart slamming against my ribs and my knees knocking together, I can barely hear it."

Alec had waited in the doorway, but now he came toward her.

She turned away, pretending to get another towel. Pressing the thumb and index finger of her right hand over her eyes, she tried to stop the tears. Crying wouldn't help anything, any more than a damn pill would.

"I just need to be alone for a few minutes," she said.

Instead of leaving, he reached out and cupped her shoulders, the heat of his palms penetrating her T-shirt. Until that moment, she hadn't realized just how cold she was.

"You need to be easier on yourself."

He turned her toward him, his right hand sliding along her shoulder and coming to rest against the side of her neck. Just as it had earlier, her pulse beat heavy and hard against the warm pad of his thumb.

Closing her eyes, she let herself just feel. She licked her dry lower lip and then swallowed unsteadily. Time stretched, and the fear of moments earlier faded, her awareness shifting toward the man who touched her. Several inches separated their bodies, but she could feel him. The hard muscles of his chest, the taut ones of his abdomen, the tension that had seemed to crackle even more strongly between them since the kiss yesterday…

His fingers trembled subtly, but he didn't remove them. Instead, his thumb moved upward to rest just in front of her ear.

Her lungs shut down for several seconds, as she waited in the dark abyss for the next sensation.

Then he stroked the line of her jaw, the action forcing her to lift her chin. A soft, guttural moan escaped from deep inside her.

"Katie?"

She opened her eyes, and for the first time glimpsed what lay beneath the controlled surface of Alec Blade. Raw heat and something so primitive and elemental that she couldn't name it.

If he ever let go, the storm would lay waste to all in its path, or take a woman someplace she'd never dreamed of going.

A place she suddenly realized that she wanted to go. With this man.

Her lips parted and her gaze focused on Alec's mouth as it descended toward hers. Inhaling roughly, she closed her eyes to wait.

Alec suddenly pulled back and stepped away. Opening her eyes, she saw the reason. Betty stood in the doorway. "I didn't mean to interrupt. I just came to see if you were all right."

Katie tried a smile but knew it was shaky at best. "I'm fine," she said as she shoved her feet back into her shoes. "I'll be right out."

As Betty turned away, Katie didn't know what to feel— irritation or relief. She glanced up at Alec as she slipped past him, but his eyes were once more dark and unreadable.

Chapter Nine

Alec turned on the desk lamp and sat down. Katie was in the other room painting, which gave him a few moments to look over what the investigator had couriered up from Miami.

Shadows remained tucked into the tall corners of the large room, but light poured onto the two manila envelopes he'd placed on his desk earlier, purposely leaving them until now.

He liked working at night. He found it easier to concentrate in the dense quiet. When he'd been with the FBI and had been called in by a local PD to provide a profile, he would sometimes take a copy of the case file, including photos, back to his hotel room. He'd put in a wake-up call for 3:00 a.m. Often the lost sleep paid off.

He slid out the jacketed report detailing Carlos's background and his movements before he'd fallen out of sight.

Taking a sip of red wine, Alec lifted the front cover. The enclosed photos were fairly generic and showed Carlos entering the gallery, then eating lunch with another man, the man's back to the camera, Carlos coming out of the grocery store. All normal activities. He was obviously of Hispanic descent, had the dark, good looks, the lean body. It wasn't surprising that Katie had found him attractive.

He found his thoughts shifting to this morning and the look in Katie's eyes when she'd believed Carlos had just walked into the restaurant. She'd been damned frightened. Was there something she hadn't told him about Carlos?

He took another sip of wine. The report seemed fairly basic and showed Carlos as pretty much an average citizen—at least as far as Miami's law enforcement was concerned. Just a few speeding and parking tickets and one assault charge three years ago shortly after he'd moved to Miami, the victim a male bar patron.

Before that move, Carlos had owned an art gallery in San Francisco where he hadn't been such a model citizen. He'd collected battery charges on a fairly regular basis, the victims always women. He'd either had a good lawyer or managed to buy his way out of doing any jail time.

As in Miami, he'd managed to have it all. Successful gallery, house overlooking the bay and a well-known artist to support both. Evidently, Katie wasn't the first woman Carlos had used.

Alec held up the photo of Carlos's most recent digs. The shot, taken from the water side, featured a large yacht as well as a three-story modern house. The good life. Was that what Katie had been looking for?

Alec fiddled with the stem of the wineglass. He couldn't seem to keep his mind on the report and off the woman.

Getting involved now was out of the question, and later might not be possible, either. He doubted Katie would stay in Deep Water. It wasn't as if she had any ties to the town. He, on the other hand, was staying. The progress on rebuilding a relationship with his brother was slow going, but he was committed to mending the rift. In the past, he'd put family last too often. He wasn't going to do that this time.

He opened a second large manila envelope, this one sent

by Seth Killian. Though the FBI had no official interest in the investigation of Jill Blade's death, Seth, who was with the FBI's Philadelphia field office and a close friend since their days at Quantico, continued to stay in touch with the lead detective on the case.

Alec had sent off a length of the surgical tubing from Katie's place for comparison with what had been used in Philadelphia. He scanned the report, focusing on the most important piece of information. The tubing was made by a well-known manufacturer of surgical supplies and was found in most physicians' offices, as well as hospitals and blood banks, but it wasn't a match to what had been knotted around Jill's ankles and wrists.

Not a match?

Alec raked both hands through his hair, and, leaning back, closed his eyes, mentally running through the list yet another time. Same brand of box cutter and candles. The method of entry—a French door with an inadequate dead bolt—was the same. As were the roses—generic long-stemmed red ones that could have been purchased almost anywhere, but to date the Central Florida vendor hadn't been located. And then there was the surgical tubing, identical diameter, but different maker. Significant?

Maybe. Maybe not. It was just as likely the killer's source had changed brands and the killer was unaware of the difference.

Alec was just sliding the report back into the envelope when Katie placed a fresh glass of wine on the corner of his desk. "I opened a new bottle." She spoke around the pencil she held between her teeth. She clutched a large sketch pad tucked under her right arm. "I hope you don't mind."

He liked that she was comfortable enough in his home to help herself, but she'd had one glass before dinner and had taken a second with her to her studio. Making the one she carried number three.

"No. But you should take it easy. Alcohol screws with more than the judgment. It also inhibits the REM phase of sleep."

"I'd have to fall asleep for that to happen."

He'd known she hadn't slept well the night before, because he'd been awake, too. And because there had been dark circles beneath her eyes this morning. "Maybe you should skip the wine and take the Valium instead."

"I don't need drugs."

He took a sip. "But you do need sleep."

She frowned as if she felt he was bullying her. "I'll sleep when this is over."

Turning away, she carried her sketch pad and her own glass of wine toward the far end of the couch. She wore loose-fitting navy blue jogging shorts and a pale pink T-shirt, and, as they often were, her feet were bare.

She flipped on the lamp on the side table. Sitting, she tucked her legs beneath her like a teenager at a slumber party.

She had no sooner propped the pad in her lap than the cat jumped up and settled beside her.

"If he bothers you, kick him off."

She ran a hand down the cat's back. "Are you allergic to cats?"

The question seemed an odd one. "No. Why would you think that?"

"Because you avoid petting him." She continued to rub the underside of the cat's chin. The animal watched Alec with a smug stare, like a criminal who knew he'd just beaten the system.

"One of Jill's students gave him to her. We didn't exactly hit it off. Even from the beginning, my only function was to throw food in a dish if she wasn't around. Otherwise, I was off his radar."

"But you kept him after…" Her words dwindled away as if she'd only then realized what she was about to say and wasn't certain how it would be received.

He leaned back in the desk chair. "Actually, I didn't. About six weeks after the funeral, I gave him to a friend with a farm." He took a sip of wine. "When I woke up the next morning, it hit me that I'd given away one of the few living creatures who missed Jill as much as I did. But when I drove out to reclaim him, he'd disappeared." Why was he telling her any of this? Must be the wine. Or perhaps it had been too long since he'd talked to anyone about fairly inconsequential topics.

"What happened?"

"A few days later he showed up at the back door, nearly dead. He'd been hit by a car trying to get home."

As she continued to stroke the large tom, he stretched out and rolled over onto his back, giving up his belly. The cat's green eyes never left Alec, and it reminded him of the times when he hadn't been on the road, and Jill would settle in on the couch with whatever novel she was reading, or with a pile of papers to grade. The cat would always lie beside her, and periodically she'd reach out to fondle an ear or paw. Alec never joined them. Instead he had continued to work, his thoughts and energies focused on one of the many cases he was juggling at the time.

It was no wonder that she'd thought his work meant more to him than she did. Truth was, he'd figured there would be time later to show her just how important she was to him. There was a tightness in his chest that he hadn't experienced since the day he buried her. He frowned. What was wrong with him tonight?

Katie flipped open the pad and, propping it on her knees, looked over at him. "You don't mind, do you, being a model? I've drawn enough plants for one night."

"No. I don't mind." It gave him the perfect excuse to watch her without appearing to be rude or probing. Her pale gray eyes narrowed in concentration as she studied him. They were both observers, he realized, though they used their observations in very different ways. He found himself recalling those moments in the supply room. The way her lips had parted. The slight hitch to her breathing as their gazes had met. He liked that hitch. It did something to him every time he heard it. Made him wonder what sounds she made at other moments during lovemaking.

She glanced up. "If you have work to do, that's fine. I'm used to moving subjects."

"Like the boy and father on surfboards?"

"Yeah." She picked up the wine. "I especially like to do kids. It pays well, but more importantly, I've never had a seven-year-old tell me that I've made a mistake in the size of his nose."

He smiled even as he slid Seth's report back in the top drawer with Jill's photos. As always, he locked the drawer, and then settled back to enjoy watching her.

Katie's gaze, when it lifted from the paper even briefly, was intense and focused. She had great eyes, wide-set and expressive. But it was her mouth, which was now hidden from view, that he considered her best feature. Soft, full. Quick to smile. He'd noticed that the first time she'd served him at the restaurant. Well, that wasn't completely accurate; he'd noticed her face first, then her trim, athletic body. The smile had come only seconds later, and had been the icing on the cake.

He'd worked with enough police artists to recognize

when the fast, sweeping movements of blocking out facial shape gave way to the tighter ones indicative of the finessing of cheekbones and brows and lips.

Alec pushed away the glass of wine. "The scars on your side. How did you come by them?"

She didn't look up, but lowered the pad slightly. "Car crash."

"The one that took your sister's life?" He'd obtained a copy of the initial report, so knew the cut-and-dry official version, but hoped that if he could get her to share a more personal one, it would further the developing level of trust between them.

"Yes." Her lips flattened. "And the reason I don't drive."

"Were you behind the wheel when it happened?"

"No," she answered. She'd stopped sketching completely now.

He waited, letting the silence grow in the shadowed room. A strategic pause. Experience told him that she wanted to talk, but was having a hard time doing so.

"It was late," she said finally. "About one in the morning. We'd sneaked out, which we had done a lot that summer. We usually went down to the beach to hang out. We'd take some pretty deserted roads to get there because Karen liked to drive fast. She was always pushing the limit, even when she wasn't behind the wheel."

He could picture it. Two teenage girls escaping parental bonds for a few hours....

"One minute everything was okay," she said in a voice suddenly heavy with emotion. "Then in the next we were rolling. We'd been hit broadside. I don't remember the actual impact. Or the car landing on its roof."

She averted her eyes. "I remember thinking it was okay, that we'd both been wearing safety belts. I was hanging in mine and figured Karen was also, but I couldn't see her because blood had run into my eyes. I…I couldn't seem to make my hands work enough to wipe it away." She stared at the pencil, running her fingers up and down its length repeatedly.

"Then I heard a car door slam. By that time, I had wiped the blood away and I watched the flashlight beam come closer. I remember thinking again that everything would be okay. That whoever the other driver was, they would help us."

She picked up her glass, but set it back down without taking a sip. "But I was wrong. He knelt down and looked in. He had a flashlight. When he reached in, I thought he was trying to get Karen out of her restraint, but he wasn't. He was taking her pulse. It was then that I realized she was dead."

He understood the pain he heard in her voice. The torment that remembering brought with it. He wanted to go to her, to offer her the comfort of his arms. But he wouldn't. Because he didn't trust himself to offer only comfort.

She fiddled with the pencil.

"After that, he aimed the flashlight at me. Stared straight at me with those emotionless eyes of his and said, sorry kid. And then he just left. I was still screaming and begging when he drove away."

Pausing she closed her eyes almost as if she were in physical pain. "A garbage truck spotted us the next morning."

Alec could imagine what those hours must have been like. Trapped in the sedan with her dead sister, uncertain if help would come in time for her.

"Was he apprehended?"

"Yes. They found him. It was more than two months later, though. He's serving time for vehicular homicide."

She seemed to be shading in some aspect of his portrait. "Mind if I ask you something?"

"Okay."

"How soon did people stop mentioning Jill? Stop asking how you were doing?"

"Not right away." But sooner than was healthy for him. He realized that now. He had needed to talk about Jill. Not about the investigation. Not about evidence and suspects. But about the woman she had been. The wife.

He'd called her parents once or twice, but even they had closed him down. They blamed him for what had happened, and saw his torment as something he deserved. He had seen it that way, too, at first.

"Two months," Katie said. "That's how long it was before people stopped asking. By the third month, the only person interested in Karen was the prosecuting attorney. Now, seven years later, it's as if she never existed. As if no one remembers just how smart and gutsy she was." Her lips flattened. "Except me."

"What about your parents?"

"They rarely mention her." She took a sip of her wine. "I know it's because it hurts. Dad was passionate about fishing. It was something he and Karen did together. They'd go off on Saturday mornings and wouldn't come back until nightfall, all fishy and dirty and laughing."

She was fiddling with the pencil again, but this time she stared at it, as well. "The morning after we spread her ashes, he took a sledgehammer to the boat. When he was done, he locked himself in his den for three days. We could hear him in there bawling, but nothing we said would make him open the door. By the time he did come out, my mother had removed every picture of Karen. I had become an only child."

She ducked her chin and rubbed her forehead. "Going through that again would destroy them."

He wanted to reassure her that nothing would happen

to her, but something stopped him. Maybe because she'd just bared a very painful part of her soul, and she deserved the truth.

"Listen, Katie, I'm not going to make you empty promises, but I can tell you one thing. He'll have to go through me to get to you."

Seeming to study her nearly empty glass, she grimaced. "Cheery thought." She glanced up, forced a smile. "What about you? Do you remember the last person to ask you how you were doing?"

"It's different in my case."

"In what way different?"

"We didn't have many couple friends. Most of mine barely knew Jill. And I spent very little time with hers. So no one really noticed when she was no longer there with me. Except Seth Killian. He was one of my coworkers who got to know Jill."

"Does he still ask?"

"Every time he calls," Alec said quietly.

Looking for some way to change the conversation, he stood. "I'm heading out to the kitchen. Can I get you anything?"

She picked up her empty glass. "Perhaps a bit more wine."

She'd have a headache in the morning.

The cat followed him, so Alec opened the cabinet and refilled the stainless bowl with cat food. With the first touch, the cat jerked away.

So much for any progress in their relationship. Alec had long ago decided the animal only stayed because he was waiting for Jill to come home.

Having put on coffee for himself, he returned to the living room with Katie's wine. He'd changed to a smaller glass and had filled it exactly half-full—enough that it wasn't readily obvious that he was trying to control her alcohol intake.

Alec sat on the couch, leaving more than a foot between them. He held out his hand. "May I have a look?"

She passed the sketch pad to him. "It's not quite finished."

He studied the drawing. Was that how she saw him? His expression grim? Eyes that seemed more probing than interested. Maybe she did. Because that's who he was.

He glanced over at her. "As I said before, and as you know, you're quite good."

"Thanks." Taking the pad, she folded it closed and placed it on the table.

While he'd been gone, she'd propped her feet on the ottoman and now rubbed the top of the left one with the toes of her right.

"Are the feet any better?" he asked. At least it was a safe subject.

Bending forward, she rubbed the instep of one, grimacing as she did it. "I wouldn't have thought five days was long enough for me to forget just how important good shoes are to a waitress." She moved on to the other one briefly before leaning back again. "I just hope I can walk in the morning."

Putting down his glass, he sat forward. "Maybe I can help. I'm pretty good at foot massages."

He understood her hesitation. They weren't exactly strangers. Nor were they really friends.

He held out his palm. "What do you have to lose? Besides sore feet?"

"If you're sure you don't mind." She swung one foot up next to his thigh. Alec lifted it into his lap, the action forcing her to reposition herself closer to him. He waited while she propped a cushion behind her.

He warmed up by rubbing her foot between his hands. "I sometimes can get carried away, so if I go at it too hard, let me know."

She smiled. "In my experience hard produces better results."

The image that came into his mind had nothing to do with foot massages.

He pulled her other foot next to the first. Starting with the instep, he worked down to where her nails were painted a pale pinky color. He spent some time working at the ball of her foot, before using the pad of his thumb on the sensitive area between her toes.

When he glanced up, she'd closed her eyes.

"Where did you learn how to do that?" she asked.

He wondered if she'd somehow known his attention had shifted from her feet to her face. "The academy."

With her eyes still shut, she smiled.

His gaze dipped to where her T-shirt draped across her breasts. No bra this time, and her nipples stood erect beneath the soft covering. As if on autopilot, his fingers continued to soothe away foot strain, but he was now envisioning them moving upward over her body, reaching the soft mounds beneath the T-shirt, massaging them gently in his palms, taking their hard peaks into his mouth...

The loose-fitting jogging shorts were pushed high on her firmly muscled thighs.

A sharp jolt of desire shot through him. Only twenty minutes ago, he'd assured himself that he could handle any attraction, and yet here he was, his pulse kicking harshly, his body ready for an act that he couldn't allow to take place.

And all because he'd opened his mouth and offered a quickie massage.

"An interrogation technique?" she asked, breaking into his line of thought.

"One of the more successful ones."

He ran his palm upward along her silky shin to her knee, then around to grasp the thicker muscle of her calf. He flexed her foot up, stretching out the tightness he felt. Eyes closed, she groaned softly and lifted her hips as his fingers worked.

Talk about the king of bad ideas. All he could think about was the smooth, satiny flesh of her thighs, the loose-fitting shorts...

She opened her eyes as he finished the second leg. "Thank you."

"You're welcome," he said as he retreated to his desk.

Katie swung her legs over the edge of the couch and sat up. She flexed her toes, almost as if someone had given her a new set of feet to try out and she was testing them.

"You can't even begin to imagine how much better that feels." She looked up at him. "The least I can do is return the favor."

What was she suggesting? That she would massage his feet? Imagining her kneeling in front of him, her hands working...

Alec picked up the pen that rested in the middle of the blotter and propped it back in the rosewood holder. "My feet are great."

She stood and moved toward him. "Of course they are. But you've been rubbing your neck and moving your shoulders as if the muscles are all knotted up."

"You're tired," he said.

The last thing he wanted was to have her hands on him. Turnabout wasn't fair play, it was dangerous play.

"And you won't be able to get to sleep all knotted up

like that." She set her empty wineglass on the desk. "I've never been very good at being a taker. Being in someone else's debt makes me uncomfortable."

"But I'm fine."

She folded her arms. "My mistake, then." Her mouth tightened momentarily and then relaxed into resignation as she turned to pick up the wineglass again.

What was wrong with him? It was just a simple neck massage.

"Maybe you're right," he said. "I do feel a bit tight."

Leaving the wineglass on the desk, she stepped behind him. Her fingers dug into his trapezius, her movements surprisingly strong and aggressive.

He refrained from closing his eyes, afraid of the images that would once again turn his body rock hard. As it was, it would take a long icy shower to cool him down. And even that might not be enough.

"I sometimes spend too much time at the easel, and this always helps me. There's a beauty shop just around the corner from my house that has a massage therapist. I just run over and let her work out all the kinks."

Obviously, they were dealing with different kinks.

He allowed his chin to drop toward his chest, giving her free reign. Maybe by making it easier for her, she'd get done sooner.

As she bore down, he could feel the slightest brush of her breasts against his back, and with each touch, the tightness in his groin increased.

He was relieved when she finally lifted her hands.

"Much better," he commented.

He started to stand, but she stalled him with a touch on his shoulder. "We're only halfway there."

Maybe she was.

She rotated the chair so that he now faced her. Quickly releasing the top few buttons of his shirt as if she was accustomed to undressing him, she pushed it aside. "You're very tight here," she said.

Using her thumbs, she massaged his deltoid.

He watched her face as she worked. Her delicate jaw tightened at the same moment her fingers did, and then briefly loosened when she shifted their position on his body. She'd taken a shower after dinner, and the scent of shampoo drifted around him. She was petite. Most people would simply overlook the supple strength of her body, the determined light in her eyes.

His lungs tightened and he closed his eyes, afraid she'd see just how turned-on he was right now.

Her breath fanned his face just before her lips settled over his.

With the first touch, he opened his eyes and met hers.

Her pupils were dilated. Her breathing was as fast and as irregular as his. But it was her mouth that he couldn't seem to ignore. Soft lips gently parted.

"This isn't a good idea," he managed, his voice roughened with restrained desire.

"No, it isn't." The tip of her tongue moistened her bottom lip. Eyes wide-open, she lowered her mouth once more until it covered his. All the while, she watched him with eyes that were honest. Trusting. Inviting.

She was vulnerable. He shouldn't take advantage. She saw him as her white knight. He wasn't. Far from it. If he'd still been with the Bureau, he would lose his job. But he wasn't. And the only job he had now was keeping her safe.

A physical relationship was still out of the question. He needed to stay focused, something he was already having problems with whenever he was around her. A physical relationship between the two of them would only cloud issues more.

And then she moaned, and he realized he was no longer listening to reason.

Instead of staying chair bound, he came to his feet, Katie straightening with him. This time, when he touched the seam of her lips with his tongue, she opened for him and he plunged. His body shuddered with raw physical need, and twisting his fingers into the cool silkiness of her hair, he deepened the kiss.

She tasted so damn good. He slid his left hand along her rib cage, his thumb just brushing the outside swell of her breast before settling at her waist. Male instinct ordered him to pull her tight against his arousal. Instead, he shoved aside the papers on his desk, magazines and several bills sliding to the floor. He lifted her so she sat on the cleared surface.

As he stepped in closer, she was forced to spread her knees. She rested her hands on his chest. He could feel his heart slamming against the curled fingers of her hand. She lifted her gaze to his and he fell in.

His fingers skimmed across her flushed cheeks. When they got to her mouth, she opened for him and his thumb slipped inside. Immediately her lips closed around him.

Damn. She was sexy. All he wanted to do was bury himself inside her, to feel her body moving beneath his.

Breathing hard now, as if he'd just finished a five-mile sprint, he eased her down onto the desk, his body hard and ready.

Katie reached for him, and it was only then that he saw the clear plastic wrapper, the kind the U.S. Postal Service used to enclose mail damaged by their machinery, on the edge of the desk, the only thing that hadn't fallen to the floor.

Even before he turned it over, he knew the card would contain only a single word.

Remember.

And the timing couldn't be any more perfect. It had shown up on the very day that he'd almost managed to forget.

Chapter Ten

The morning air held the unseasonably crisp promise of fall. Alec, in a hurry to find his brother, pushed through the crowd surrounding Deep Water Spring's century-old wooden bandstand, where senate hopeful Paul Darby was to appear in less than thirty minutes.

Red, white and blue banners snapped in the sharp breeze. Most of the audience seemed to have dressed for the weather, and those who hadn't were congregated in areas where either the sunshine poured through a break in the oak canopy, or where one of the news vans—the only kind that had been allowed into the immediate area— afforded them a buffer from wind gusts.

Alec was supposed to have met Jack at the café to turn over the postcard, but there had been some last-minute security issues for the rally that had required Jack's immediate attention. From the look of it, Jack must have pulled in every available officer to cover the event.

It was beginning to appear as if the only cop left back in town was the one who had been eating breakfast when Alec had dropped Katie at the restaurant. Even though he'd promised to stick around until Alec returned, the damned truth was that Alec didn't trust anyone with Katie's safety.

Though he was determined not to think about what had happened last night—not just the kiss, but also the way he'd lost control—he couldn't seem to stop himself. Another three seconds, and he would have had both of them naked.

He shoved his fingers into his hair. Lunacy. That's all it was.

The crowd suddenly opened up, and he found himself face-to-face with Jolie Kennedy, WKMG's top investigative reporter. She was dressed in her on-air clothes, a red suit and heels, so he assumed her mike to be live.

"Alec Blade, is it true that the recent attack on a local woman may have been committed by the same man who murdered your wife nearly a year ago?"

"No comment." He'd said those words so many times in his career that they were like breathing. Fresh air in, stale air out. Reporter asks a question on a subject that you haven't had a chance to analyze fully, canned response. Anything else was dangerous. To the victim, to the investigation and to the likelihood of your continued employment.

He tried stepping around the brunette reporter, but the several dozen people who had been within earshot when she'd posed the question now created a wall of resistance, not only with their bodies, but also with their hard stares.

When he allowed his gaze to connect to Jolie's, she smiled, and he could see the predatory excitement there. She knew she had him cornered.

"Don't you think the people have a right to know that your presence in this town has placed them in danger? And that Deep Water's police chief—your brother—has conspired to keep this very real threat from the public?"

He kept his expression bland. "All we have right now is an assault victim." We? He realized too late that he'd spoken as if he were involved in the investigation on a professional basis. Certainly not the impression he wanted to give. "The public is not in any danger, and I can assure you that if they were, Chief Blade would take all necessary steps to rectify the situation."

He briefly scanned the crowd, looking for Jack, but then quickly returned his attention to the reporter. "Maybe you should check the statistics. Deep Water has less crime today than when my brother took over the position."

The wind tugged at Jolie's open jacket and forced the thin, white silk blouse to hug her breasts and narrow rib cage. She was one of those women who were better-looking on screen than off.

She stared up at him, a smug expression overtaking her features. "Well, maybe you can at least comment on this. How does it feel to know that one woman has already died because of her association with you, and that another one may face the same fate?"

It was a common interrogation technique. If a reporter asked a question often enough, from enough different angles, sometimes she got lucky. Not this time, though.

"Maybe you shouldn't read so much fiction," Alec said. "Now if you'll excuse me."

He no sooner broke through the crowd than he saw Jack, who motioned for him to follow.

"What's going on?" Alec asked. "Why all the officers?"

"Darby's campaign manager called this morning. He received another threat last night. Placed from a stolen cell phone. Nothing specific. Just a you'll-be-sorry."

Alec realized his brother was headed for the staging area just behind the platform. With the roped-off section keeping the crowd at bay, they were alone except for the odd officer cutting through, or one of the politician's point men making a last-minute check before Darby's arrival.

Alec was already trying to analyze the fallout from what had just taken place. If the interview made the six o'clock news, more reporters would be looking into a possible connection between Jill's death and Katie's assault. Eventually there would be no dodging the truth, and any hope of luring the killer into making a move became that much more difficult.

"How do you think she found out about the connection to Jill?" Jack asked, obviously having heard the reporter's question. "It didn't come from anywhere inside my force."

"She's just fishing at this point. That doesn't mean she won't get enough to make a story. Even by tonight."

As he pulled the postcard from his pocket, still sealed in the plastic and now enclosed in a white envelope, he couldn't help but think about the typed word on its back. *Remember.* After receiving eleven of them, he would have expected it to get easier, but it hadn't. *Remember.* That single word held him in the past, kept him desperately searching death-row cases where he'd played a part, kept him reliving the night he'd come home to find his wife dead.

And yet this crinkled card with two of its four corners ripped away might provide them with the break they needed.

He passed it to his brother. "All the automatic sorter left for us to work with is the message and a Deep Water postmark. With any luck, maybe someone saw it being mailed."

"I'll let you know what I find out." Jack ran the long edge of the envelope through his index finger and thumb. "You said the postmark was the twentieth, right? Just like the others?"

"Yes." Alec noticed an attractive fiftysomething woman

in the crowd staring in their direction and realized how the passing of the envelope might look to an outsider. "Perhaps you should put that away."

Jack's gaze followed Alec's. He smiled. "Afraid the mayor's wife will think it's a payoff?"

After tossing a wave in the woman's direction, Jack tucked the envelope in his shirt pocket. "The night of Katie's assault, you seemed fairly certain that the reason you hadn't received anything in the mail was because he saw Katie as his October postcard."

"Shoots that theory to hell, doesn't it?" Alec commented.

Jack touched the pocket containing the envelope. "Did you want me to have this run through the lab for fingerprints?"

"No. Just get it back to me and I'll send it up to Philly. I don't hold out much hope, anyway."

They'd run all the previous postcards through the lab, not only looking for fingerprints but also hoping to find a match—any link—between the cards. To date they'd been unable to do either.

The crowd had nearly doubled in size, and now took up most of the clearing.

Jack plucked the radio off his belt, started to raise it to his mouth, and then lowered it. "Any chance you can give us a hand here for the next hour or so? Play backup to Darby's security team?"

Alec would have preferred to head back into town. Not to the café, of course, since they had to make it appear as if Katie had been left unprotected. But to the library down the street where he could find a quiet corner and turn on his laptop. Several keystrokes later, he would be watching everything that went on inside the restaurant and breathing a whole lot easier.

But as much as he wanted to say no, it was the first time Jack had asked a professional favor of him. "Sure."

"Miss?" The man who had picked up the broken dishes yesterday morning motioned for a coffee refill by raising his mug.

Katie was on her way to pick up an order, but stopped with the nearly empty carafe in her hand. "They just put on another pot." She poured the mug only half-full. "I'll bring you some fresh in a minute."

"This is fine. I'm already late as it is." He glanced out the front window as another gust of wind buffeted the plate glass. "That wind picks up much more and we'll have some trees and power lines down."

Usually, by this time of morning, foot traffic filled the sidewalk and women eager to get out of the house with their young children crowded the park benches across the bricked street.

But not today. Laishley Park was deserted except for what was probably a couple of college kids attempting to launch a kite. It had been nearly two weeks since she had ventured over there. She missed sketching the children at play, seeing the face of a mother light up when she offered her the sketch.

"The winds are supposed to die by tonight," she commented, having listened to the news on the way in.

The last time she'd seen this man, he'd been dressed in nice slacks and a dress shirt, but today he wore a work shirt, blue jeans and well-used cowboy boots. Which surprised her because he didn't really look like the outdoor type.

"You work around here?" She glanced at the wall clock behind the register. Nine o'clock. Where was Alec? He was to have dropped off the postcard, and then come back for breakfast.

When she looked back down, the customer was watching her over the rim of his mug.

He set the coffee down slowly. "Yes. Just started out at the Barnetts' place."

It took her half a beat to realize that he was answering the question she'd asked before her thoughts had become distracted. Barnett place? Was that a ranch?

She scooped up the used creamer packaging and the empty sugar packet. "Well, I hope we'll be seeing a lot of you in here."

A well-dressed woman at the next table caught her attention. "Miss, we've been waiting for our check for more than five minutes."

Katie touched the table edge. "Excuse me."

She stopped at the other table. "I'll send Betty right over with your check." With one hand still holding the coffeepot, she could only clear away one of the plates.

The restaurant was busier than usual for a Tuesday morning. Most of the locals discussed the political rally, while the few tourists who had found their way to the Alligator Café talked about theme parks and beaches. Neither group's conversation managed to catch much of her attention.

She kept replaying the scene from the previous night over and over in her head, and cringing inside a bit more with each rerun. She'd actually been the aggressor. Oh, sure, her defenses were down. The half bottle of merlot was part of the problem. And then there had been the conversation about her sister, which had left her feeling more emotionally vulnerable than she had in years.

Those excuses might work if he'd been the one to make the first move. But he hadn't been. She had.

Her abdominal muscles tightened as if his hands were once more moving over her skin. Strong fingers. A firm pressure. The hands of a man who knew what he was capable of doing to a woman. He would be a demanding lover, the kind that would push a woman to her limits, and then, when she didn't think there was any more left, he would take her even further.

Not that she was ever going to know.

She swiped the damp rag across the cleared table, moving aside the salt and pepper shakers to wipe up what appeared to be spilled syrup.

As she straightened, the rag still clutched in her hand, she recalled the moment everything had gone to hell, the moment Alec picked up something from the corner of the desk. Almost as if it had been left there by some divine hand.

The postcard.

She knew about the postcard that came every month. But as he had slowly turned over the card last night, the quickly buried flash of pain in his gray eyes, the fingers that had trembled as they held the card… It had told her just how hard not just the twentieth of each month, but every day on a calendar must be for Alec. Each day that went by brought him closer to another postcard. To another reminder.

How did he survive? If the man responsible for Karen's death hadn't gone to prison, she wouldn't have been able to stand it. Knowing he was walking free while her sister's ashes had been scattered to the winds….

Last night, she would have done anything to ease Alec's pain, but there had been nothing she could do. She'd been where he was right now.

Just as she'd had to forgive herself for being the daughter who had survived, Alec was going to have to find some way to forgive himself. It wasn't what others told you about yourself; it was what you believed deep down inside your own soul that mattered the most.

And deep down in his, he still blamed himself for Jill's death.

She glanced up as a couple with three kids walked in. They were all dressed in shorts and theme park sweatshirts, probably hastily bought when the temperatures had taken a downturn. She offered them a smile, and, grabbing menus, seated them in her section.

The next hour passed quickly, but each time the front door opened, she looked toward it, expecting to see Alec, becoming more and more worried when she didn't. She knew he had a cell phone, but she didn't have the number. There hadn't been any reason for her to get it. He was always going to be just down the street. Thirty seconds away. But now she didn't know where he was, and because she didn't, she was nervous.

She'd just given out individual checks to a party of twelve ladies. The other two waitresses working the shift had already left. With only four tables still occupied—none of them hers and all but one regulars in the restaurant— Katie caught Betty's attention and motioned that she needed a five-minute reprieve.

If nothing else, on the way home tonight, she was going to get her work shoes. She wasn't going another day without Rockports.

She flicked on the supply room's light fixture as she entered and immediately kicked off her shoes. It hadn't been much more than twenty-four hours since Alec had followed her in here.

What was wrong with her?

She rubbed her forehead. Getting involved with a man who obviously still had strong feelings for his dead wife was asking for trouble. She knew that. Just as she knew any relationship between them was destined to be short-lived. If they were successful in catching this guy, when it was all over, she would just be a reminder of Jill. And he would be a reminder of a horrific time in her life. Getting on with their respective lives would be easier without those reminders.

But that didn't stop her from wanting him.

She jerked her purse down from an upper shelf and plopped it on a lower one. The Valium bottle somehow had made its way to the top of the bag. Maybe the work of the same divine hand that had delivered the postcard last night.

Shoving the container aside, she dug out one peppermint stick—a leftover from last Christmas that she tossed immediately into the trash can five feet away—and had just corralled a roll of spearmint Life Savers, when a quick flash of reflected light bounced off a large soup pot just to her right. No. Not bounced off, but the light that came down the narrow hall from the dining room had been briefly blocked as someone entered the hallway.

It was probably just Betty. She'd pretend to be checking on Katie, but what she really wanted was to question her about Alec—a subject Katie had been dodging all morning.

"I'll be right there," she called over her shoulder and went back to peeling out a candy.

The hairs at the back of her neck suddenly lifted, as if a cold hand had caressed her spine. The barely discernable sound of cloth brushing across cloth reached her at the same time as she saw a murky silhouette in the highly polished surface of the pot. Not Betty, but a man's broad shoulders.

Her fingers suddenly stilled as the door clicked closed. Slowly, she removed her hand from the purse and as nonchalantly as possible reached for the only weapon she saw. A can of green beans.

Why here?

Why now, when even if he managed to kill her, there was little chance he'd get away with it?

Alec's words came back to her with sudden clarity. *If he's willing to pay the ultimate price…*

AT JACK'S REQUEST, Alec lingered in the staging area. But he would have preferred to have been sitting in the library, a quick sprint from Katie.

He wasn't expecting anything to happen just yet. As an organized thinker, their guy would want to study the situation. Before he acted, he would need to determine the safest and the cleanest way to get to his target.

At least that's what Alec had believed until last night… until the postcard had come. Now, he wasn't so certain.

Was their guy slowly coming unglued, just as Bundy had those last weeks in Florida? Some believed Bundy had headed to Florida—a state where the death penalty still existed—because he wanted to be stopped. Up until that time, he'd been so careful that even those closest to him had never suspected anything. And then suddenly, he seemed to spiral down, almost as if some force—God or a more internal demon—drove him to expose himself to greater risk.

Alec prayed that was not what was happening with Jill's killer. Because if it was, Alec was about to find himself in uncharted territory.

As soon as the white limousine delivered Paul Darby at nine forty-five, the media swarmed, and it was left to the police officers to keep them at bay.

Prominent local citizens, including the mayor's wife, were already seated on the bandstand. The high school band, positioned just to the right of the structure, announced the politician's arrival on stage as did an equal number of cheers and boos.

Alec caught sight of Jack moving through the crowd.

Following an introduction given by a party leader, Darby bounded to the podium, one hand raised in the air, almost as if claiming victory even before the polls opened.

Like most speeches given by politicians, there was a lot of plate decoration and not much to sink your teeth into. After the first few minutes, Alec tuned out Darby's voice and focused on the crowd. As he scanned the audience, he evaluated each face.

"Off the record—"

Alec glanced down at Jolie Kennedy. He'd seen her working her way toward him absent the mike and the cameraman. "No comment." He returned his attention to the crowd.

"The public has the right to know."

"And it's your mission to tell them?"

She shoved the hair away from her eyes. "That's right."

He looked down at her. "If you'll excuse me," he said and stepped toward the bandstand. The politician's security team had remained fairly stationary, but now was on the move. Two out of the three men were newly hired—probably more for their bulk than their brains— and looked to the third, a seasoned veteran, for direction.

And right now, eager to complete his assigned job so he could get back to town and Katie, Alec intended to do everything in his power to make sure the politician got to his limo without incident.

What was scheduled to be an hour-long production had just been shortened to a twenty minute super stop. Just enough to demonstrate that the politician was fearless, that he wasn't going to let a few threats throw him off stride.

Those positioned inside the ropes as he descended the steps—people with media passes or with some connection to Darby's political party—held out hands that were shaken without hesitation.

The seasoned member of the security team shadowed his employer, protecting his back, and at the same time attempted to direct the younger members of the team to open up a path leading to the car.

Everything was going along as planned, and then Darby suddenly turned and went for the audience. People surged to meet him, and in the process cut off even Darby's experienced bodyguard, who was left to flounder upstream against a current of humanity.

Not that the politician seemed to notice. He waded forward, and because of the way he used both hands simultaneously to shake those on either side of him, it almost looked as if he was being pulled toward the center of the crowd.

Alec had been debating if he should sit tight, when he caught a sudden movement off to the right.

A man forced his way through the audience, obviously headed for the politician. Large. Wearing a navy blue baseball cap with yellow lettering and a jean jacket. The man looked up, his gaze briefly meeting Alec's across the sea of heads, and as it did, Alec knew the trouble everyone had been hoping to avoid was just moments from happening.

With no other choice, he plunged forward. People gave him dirty looks as he shoved his way past them. The comments in his wake weren't any nicer. He briefly lost track of the man. When Alec again located him, he realized the man was going to reach Darby before Alec could.

No sign of a weapon yet, but that could mean that he was smart enough not to show it too early.

A tandem baby stroller suddenly cut off Alec's route. After only the briefest hesitation, he went over it. The look of outrage on a tall blond woman who had been standing in the general vicinity of the contraption told him that she was the mother. Without stopping, he threw an apology over his shoulder.

It was definite now. He wasn't going to make it. And neither were any of Darby's security people.

It was then that Alec saw the gun come out of the man's pocket. He was still a dozen feet from Darby when a cowboy-type realized what was happening and tackled the man from behind, the forward momentum taking down Darby and those standing nearest him like a full rack of bowling pins.

By the time Alec got there, Darby was climbing to his feet, helped by two of Jack's officers. He was escorted to the waiting limo. The suspect took the same route several seconds later, blackened eyes downcast, and his split lip still bleeding.

Alec looked at the audience member who'd made the tackle. Six-two. A clean-shaven head that seemed to accentuate his heavy features.

"Nice moves," he said and held out his hand.

The guy grinned as they shook. "Thanks. I played center in high school."

Joining them, Jack extended his hand to the cowboy. "Thanks for jumping in. The bad news now is, as a citizen who was willing to get involved when the situation required it, you get the privilege of spending the next hour or so with one of my deputies."

The man nodded. "I don't have anywhere to be for a few hours."

"Well, I do." Alec was already backing away.

TWENTY MINUTES LATER, Alec burst through the Alligator Café's front door. Café owner Pete Repete was busy at the register, checking out half a dozen women.

Alec did a quick scan of the dining room. Two sets of couples were seated near the front window. A third table held what looked to be a newly delivered plate of eggs and bacon, but no diner. Probably went to the restroom.

And there was no sign of the police officer who was supposed to be watching Katie.

Alec stepped into the narrow kitchen. The place was spotless, even the old linoleum floor tiles, but as in most breakfast joints there was an overriding scent of grease and cold dishwater. The cook, a young kid from Fort Myers, was scraping down the griddle, while the busboy loaded one of two commercial dishwashers.

"Where's Katie?"

Both men shrugged, but it was the cook who spoke. "Haven't seen her since things slowed down out front."

He'd told her to stay with people, to stay visible. "What about the police officer who was here earlier?"

Both men shrugged again. Alec hurried out of the kitchen and toward the supply room. He'd made a bad judgment call, entrusting Katie's safety to someone else. It was his promise, his responsibility to be certain that nothing happened to her.

The third table, the one with the fresh plate, the untouched cup of coffee, was still unoccupied. It had been too long for a restroom break.

He stopped just inside the hall and drew his weapon. The supply room door was closed. She could just be changing her T-shirt. There might be nothing wrong.

Katie screamed, and was still screaming when Alec kicked in the door.

The man—Alec recognized him as someone who had

been in the restaurant recently—had Katie pinned in the corner. The contents of the overturned shelf unit, mostly cans, covered the floor.

Alec took advantage of the other man's surprise, and slammed his fist into his face. The man stumbled backward. Alec reached out and, catching him by the collar, slammed him up against the wall. The man's eyes, which had briefly closed as his head impacted the wall, doubled in size when Alec shoved the Glock in his face.

The roar inside Alec's head was like a freight train bearing down on him. He'd been waiting for this moment for eleven months, twenty-seven days and ten hours. And now it was here. In the blink of an eye, he could end it. Save the taxpayers hundreds of thousands of dollars, save him the torture of a trial where he'd have to listen as this man told of Jill's last minutes…

"Get the hell out of here, Katie!"

She didn't move.

"Now!"

"Alec, no!" Katie stumbled across the littered floor and latched on to his arm. "It's not him. He's not the one who attacked me. He's not Jill's killer."

His index finger still lying on the trigger, he looked over at her. He barely registered that her fingers were digging into his bicep.

"It's not him!" She tried to push her body between them. "You can't do this!"

Not him? Reason was like an incoming tide, overtaking him in waves. He looked at the man he held. The height might be right, but the build wasn't.

"Alec." Jack stood in the doorway. "Lower your weapon."

Chapter Eleven

"You better get your act together, Alec. And in a damn hurry!"

Jack leaned across the interrogation room table that separated them. "You're out of control."

Alec planted his hands on the table. "I would never have pulled that trigger. And you know it!"

Jack tossed down the file he'd been holding. "You're just damned lucky that you aren't being booked on assault charges right now!" Jack stabbed a finger at the interrogation room's closed door. "If that man had wanted to, there would have been nothing I could do to stop him. In fact, the prosecution would have to call me as a witness." He stood, paced to the window overlooking the parking lot. "I should take away your weapon. If you were anyone else, and if the situation were different, I wouldn't hesitate."

Alec undid the shoulder holster and slammed it with the weapon still encased in leather onto the table. "Take it. I have three more—"

Jack turned back, and for a brief instant, Alec saw something that he hadn't expected to, something that made him pause. Jack looked tired and worried.

"Is something going on with you?"

Jack sat down again, and, leaning back in his chair, looked up at his brother. "Take your weapon, Alec. And take some advice, too. Back off. Off of the responsibility that you feel for Jill's death, off of whatever is happening between you and Katie."

"Nothing's happening."

Jack shook his head, and briefly looked away as if choosing his next words. "We both know there's no room in law enforcement for emotions."

Alec gave a sharp nod. "You're right, there isn't. But there's no walking away, either. Not until it's finished." He straightened.

The harsh words Jack had thrown around earlier lost all power as his gaze met Alec's. "Just make sure it doesn't finish you."

Alec's eyes narrowed. "I'll be careful."

Alec was almost to the door, when Jack spoke. "I'll need you to make a statement about what happened out at the park this morning."

"Sure." He turned. "Have you learned anything yet?"

"Name's Ralph Henry, and he blames politicians like Darby for the loss of his construction company. Jack walked around the table. "Do you plan to send Katie back to the restaurant?"

"That depends on Jolie Kennedy. If she runs any kind of story, it won't be just a killer looking for Katie, but every damn journalist and reporter, too. She'll have to go back in hiding."

"But will she?" Jack asked.

"I don't know. She's a very determined lady." Alec opened the door. He frowned. Something was bothering Jack. "You're sure things are okay with you?"

"Yeah. I'm sure."

SHIELDED INSIDE Jack's office, Katie watched with a sense of embarrassment as the man from the restaurant's supply room disappeared down the hall. He'd just wanted to ask her out on a date.

Score one for the crazy woman with the can of green beans.

But it wasn't funny, was it? In those moments before Alec had kicked in the door, she'd thought she was going to die. But even more frightening were those that had followed his arrival. The cold look in Alec's eyes as he'd held a gun to another man's head.

She tightened her arms across herself.

How could Alec, who had looked at her with such warmth and compassion last night, be the same man who had been in that supply room? Filled with enough hate that he could take another man's life without hesitation?

The door opened, and she turned toward it. Alec stood in the opening. For the first time her eyes were wide open when she looked at him.

She no longer saw him as he'd been depicted in the articles she'd read online. Not as a hero who willingly crawled into the minds of killers. But as a man capable of the same violence as the men he hunted. She'd been stunned by his aggression. Really shaken.

For several seconds neither of them said anything. Maybe Alec sensed that she was having a hard time coping with what had happened.

"Are you ready to leave?" he said from where he still stood near the door.

She nodded but made no move in his direction.

What now? Did she share the thoughts spinning through her head? Or keep her mouth shut?

Alec closed the door behind him. "What's wrong?"

"Nothing." She turned away. Now was the wrong time to make a decision. She needed to think it through first.

"You want out? Is that what you want?"

Tightening her arms across herself, she paced to the opposite end of the room. Did she? Alec had said she only had to say the words. But what then?

She faced him. "No. But I do want to know if you lied to keep me in Deep Water. I want to know exactly how far you would go, Alec, to get Jill's killer."

He didn't say anything for several long moments. "Not that far."

His eyes were as cold now as they had been this morning. Only this time the anger was directed at her.

"That's not what it looked like this morning," she said. "It looked as if you were willing to go to hell and back to see Jill's killer dead. Damn the consequences. And whoever got in your way."

"Hell and back?" A dry chuckle followed those words. "I'm in hell and there's no going back."

He walked slowly toward her. "Do you know what real hell is? I'll tell you. Jill came to me six weeks before her death. She claimed she was being stalked. I didn't do anything. Didn't even check it out. You want to know why? Because I didn't believe her. She'd accused me so many times before of neglecting our marriage that I figured the story was just another attempt to get my attention. So what do I do? I book a ten-day cruise. Just a pat on the head instead of taking the time to really listen. I had the tickets in my pocket that night when I climbed those stairs and found her. So do I hold her killer responsible? Yes. I do. But I hold myself more responsible. I had vowed to cherish and protect. I did neither."

Even the hard look in his eyes couldn't conceal his

torment. She'd known that he blamed himself for not being there that night, but this was more horrible than she'd imagined. She tried to envision how she would feel if she'd been behind the wheel the night Karen had died.

"You made a mistake."

"No, Katie. A mistake is forgetting an anniversary or to pick up the dry cleaning. There is no excuse for what I did. Just ask Jill's parents."

"They're just hurting. In time they'll—"

Without waiting for her to finish, he turned on his heel and headed for the door. "If you want out, Katie, I'll hire the bodyguard and do whatever else it takes to keep you safe." He opened the door. "Right now, Martinez will take you home and stay with you."

"And where will you be?"

"In Orlando, talking a station manager out of running a story."

IT WAS SIX O'CLOCK when Alec took I-4 east toward Deep Water. It had taken him more than three hours to convince WKMG's station manager to pull the story temporarily. Jolie had stormed out shortly after Alec's arrival, leaving him worried that despite her contract with WKMG she may have gone to another station with what she had.

If the story broke, they'd lose the best shot they had of apprehending Jill's killer.

And that was assuming Katie even wanted to continue.

Every time he'd called Martinez to check on her, he'd been told that she was in her studio. He would have liked more information about her state of mind, but hadn't been willing to ask Martinez outright. Which meant he'd find out when he got home.

He wasn't sure how to handle things with her. He didn't

know what was going on inside her head. The way he'd acted in the supply room had her spooked. There was no way he could tell her that when he'd kicked in that door, he hadn't been thinking about Jill. He'd been thinking about Katie. About something happening to her.

I-4 traffic suddenly slowed in front of him and then came to a complete standstill. Seconds later an ambulance and fire truck sped by using the emergency lane. For the next forty-five minutes, Central Florida's main east-west artery became a parking lot.

The steady rain of the past few hours slowed to a drizzle as he turned into Katie's subdivision. He glanced at the Explorer's outside temperature gauge. Fifty-seven. More like Pennsylvania weather than Florida.

He'd told Katie he'd come by to pick up her shoes, but now wondered if it might be a wasted trip. There was every possibility when he got home tonight that she'd tell him she wanted out. And he couldn't blame her.

Alec parked in front of the bungalow. Turning off the engine, he sat there for several minutes, watching the rain on the windshield slowly turn the dark neighborhood into a surreal scene. He was tired. And not just physically, but mentally exhausted, too. He hadn't slept well in three hundred and sixty-two nights now. Another three would mark the first anniversary.

Climbing out, he scanned the quiet streets. Front porch lights shined at regular intervals, almost like those that lined an airfield landing strip. Most would remain on throughout the night because the people inside those homes couldn't forget what had happened just down the street from them.

Katie wasn't the only victim. Deep Water itself was. The quiet town that time had seemed to forget for much of the second half of the twentieth century had been ripped into the present. And even when Jill's killer was apprehended, that wouldn't change. There was no going back.

The scent of burning leaves simmered in the air. The low hum of distant traffic and the sound of a train whistle reached him. Lonely sounds. And he admitted he had never felt lonelier than he did at that moment.

Recalling how the overgrown bushes surrounding the courtyard blocked the light from the streetlamp, he retrieved the flashlight from the glove box. Alec headed up the narrow, cracked sidewalk, scanning the beam ahead of him as he went.

Until it landed on Jolie Kennedy's body.

She was sprawled faceup, her blue eyes staring heavenward. Droplets of rain ran from their corners as if she were crying. The length of surgical tubing knotted around her neck appeared to be embedded there.

Fairly certain that it was a waste of time, Alec squatted next to her and searched for a pulse. He didn't find one, though, and her skin felt cool beneath his fingertips, suggesting that she'd been dead for at least an hour or more.

The jacket of her red pantsuit had been ripped open, exposing the pale skin of her rib cage and abdomen.

He recalled watching an interview she'd given recently. One of the network morning shows had been doing a segment on local reporters who were responsible for breaking what turned out to be top national stories the previous year. When the interviewer had questioned her about the reason she always wore the color, she'd answered without hesitation. Red suggested power, demanded attention, ketchup didn't show on it, and neither did blood—all of which were important to an investigative reporter.

As Jolie had stormed out of the station manager's office

earlier, she had screamed that nothing, not anyone, could keep her from reporting the news.

She'd been wrong. Someone had. And in the process made *her* the lead story.

"THE VULTURES HAVE ARRIVED," Jack said, drawing Alec's gaze to the two news vans that had pulled up to the curb, neither of them belonging to WKMG.

More than an hour and fifteen minutes had elapsed since he'd discovered Jolie. A crowd had formed outside the bungalow shortly after the first emergency vehicle arrived. Mostly neighbors who'd been drawn out of their homes by the strobing lights, and who had remained in spite of the steady rain.

It had been only a matter of time before the media followed.

The irony struck him. He'd spent the afternoon convincing Jolie's station manager to hold the story. Now the man's best reporter was the story, and there was no way to keep the media away.

Jack's deputies, however, kept them behind the crime tape strung out near the street.

Halogen lights had been set up, creating day out of night in the courtyard. Half a dozen techs borrowed from Orlando and Volusia County worked the scene. In another few minutes, a tarp would be erected in an attempt to keep any remaining evidence from being washed away, but Alec suspected it was already a wasted effort.

Jack turned to the investigators crawling around the overgrown bushes and yelled loud enough that all in the courtyard could hear him, "Anyone find that camera yet? It has to be here."

He glanced inside the red satchel that had been found

beside the body. It contained all the tools required by a determined investigative reporter, including ones for B and E. "Evidently she wasn't letting the law keep her from getting the story."

"Apparently not." Alec watched the medical examiner carefully wrap the body in a new white sheet, then place it in the body bag. He had his own theories about what had become of the camera. Either the killer had taken it as a souvenir, something to remember his victim by, or he'd wanted the film the camera contained. And if it was the film, why had he wanted it? Because it contained photos of him? Or had he seen the camera as a convenient opportunity to immortalize his victim?

"What do you think?" Jack asked his brother as the black bag was zipped closed. "Do you think he knew it was Jolie? Or do you think in the dark he thought it was Katie?"

"If I had to make a guess, I'd say he thought he had Katie. The height and the build are about the same. Hair color, too. By the time he discovered he had the wrong woman, it was too late." He looked over at his brother. "If anything, this is going to drive him closer to the edge."

"What do you mean?"

Alec glanced at the black bag holding the victim. A puddle formed in one of the plastic valleys. A smaller one overflowed, leaking the collected rain onto the ground.

No husband or children waiting at home. In spite of the regret he felt over her death, that's all he knew about her life. That and that she was a tenacious and resolute woman. It was those two qualities—ones that he'd always admired in other people—that had brought her here tonight to get a story, and into the path of a killer.

"I mean he'll see this as his second failure where Katie is concerned," Alec said. "The level of his frustration and hate will continue to escalate until the goal—killing Katie—will take precedence over everything, even over his own survival."

He rubbed the water off his face and stared toward the street where the crowd remained. "Is the video still running?"

"It's rolling, and I have officers working their way through the crowd and checking nearby cars. If he's there, we'll get him. As you said before, it shouldn't be too hard to pick out the face that doesn't belong." Jack's gaze followed Alec's.

The man they hunted would have a nearly uncontrollable urge to stand in the crowd, watching. He would enjoy seeing the bright lights and the men crawling across the ground. Because it allowed him to believe that he was superior to them. That he was the master. That with a mere tug on a string, he could make them all dance.

As he had tonight.

He would enjoy watching Alec, too, because, no matter how much Alec tried to conceal it, he knew he looked tired and defeated.

"What about the arrangement with Katie?" Jack asked. "Think it's time to make some changes? Perhaps stash her someplace?"

"There's no turning back." Alec ran a hand through his damp hair and tried not to think about those first few seconds after he'd found Jolie's body. When he'd thought it was Katie. "There never was." He looked over at his brother. "Katie wouldn't go, anyway. Not after this."

"Not many women would be doing what she's doing," Jack commented.

Seeing the speculation in Jack's eyes, Alec fixed his attention on the crowd again. Not many women, was right.

Jack laid a hand on Alec's shoulder. "Maybe you should go home. To Katie."

Alec shoved his hands deeper into his pockets. After what he'd said to her in Jack's office this afternoon, he doubted Katie was eager for him to return. But for a moment, he allowed himself to contemplate what it would be like to go home to her if things were right between them. Home to her quick smile and resilient nature. To her soft, supple body and warm skin. To the blinding heat of need and the warmth of physical satisfaction. But more than sex, it was the conversation, the sense of connection that he felt when he was with her that he wanted to go home to.

But he wouldn't be going home to any of those things. The only thing waiting for him was the hard job of telling a frightened woman that a killer had made a mistake, had killed another woman, all the time believing it was her.

Chapter Twelve

Alec hit the remote to open the wrought-iron gates in front of his home. He'd been listening to a jazz station out of Orlando, hoping to unwind a bit, but turned it down now as he waited for the gates to swing wide enough for the SUV.

It was past two thirty in the morning. He and half a dozen police officers, all longtime Deep Water residents, had spent the past hour and a half studying the video of the crowd outside Katie's bungalow.

Only eleven faces hadn't been quickly identified as belonging to Azalea Park neighbors. Of those, five could be eliminated due to gender or age. That left six potentials to be checked out. Chances were at least three of them owned police scanners and considered accident scenes and fires to be just another form of entertainment. The rest…well…they could have been visiting someone in the area. Or, if Alec was lucky, one of the unrecognized faces belonged to the killer.

Alec dreaded the coming confrontation with Katie. She wouldn't take the news well. She was a strong woman, but not a pragmatic one.

He'd been thinking about her more than he would have liked, but it was just chemistry. Even what had happened last night was just chemistry. He'd been without any type of physical relationship for nearly a year, and clearly, the conversation about her sister had left Katie feeling vulnerable, needy. The wine had simply done away with any remaining inhibitions for both of them.

But, no matter what the circumstances, he wouldn't have let it go any further than it had.

Alec rubbed a hand over his face. Who the hell was he trying to kid here? If he hadn't noticed the postcard on the desk, he wouldn't have stopped. He would have taken her right there. His body tightened as his mind served up images. Her lips softly swollen. Her quickened breathing as he'd slipped his fingers beneath her T-shirt. The way she'd trembled as his hand had… He shouldn't be thinking about any of those things. A woman was dead, and the fact that he couldn't seem to keep his mind firmly focused on the investigation was just another indication that he needed to build some distance from Katie.

When the gates were once more securely closed, Alec dropped the SUV back into gear.

He'd sold the Philadelphia house for more than twenty thousand below market value—a well-publicized murder tended to lower a home's marketability—and bought this white elephant of a house for what by Philadelphia standards was a reasonable amount. He hadn't really wanted the square footage as much as the privacy afforded by the acre and a half of land and the distance from town.

The place, which needed some work and a hell of a lot of furniture, had been built in the late 1890s by a naturalist. Which accounted for the large solarium at the back of the house and also explained why the extensive grounds had been left in their natural state.

He'd planned to clear away much of it, but once he'd moved in, decided not to.

Moonlight, penetrating the oak canopy, cast a lacy filigree of light onto the blacktop. As he made the last bend in the drive, he realized the light over the front door appeared to be the only illumination. Alec stopped the vehicle. Even if Katie had gone to bed, where were the signs indicating Martinez's whereabouts? Alec sat there for several seconds before dropping the car into reverse. Something wasn't right.

Leaving the SUV out of sight of the house, he slipped the automatic weapon from the shoulder holster. Moments earlier, Alec had been dead on his feet, but now adrenaline pumped through him.

The scent of wet earth permeated the night air as he moved cautiously toward the house.

Under a sharp gust of wind, palmetto fronds clacked softly. In the next instant, as the wind died, there was no disguising the sharp crack of someone or something moving through the thicket on his right. The property backed up to the wildlife preserve, so it was just as likely to be a deer as it was to be a man. But Alec stood there for several seconds listening.

There was no way to get over the tall wrought-iron fence that ran three sides of the property without tripping the alarm, leaving only the rear of the house exposed. Getting in that way undetected would be difficult, requiring a boat if you didn't want to get wet, but it wouldn't be impossible. He'd installed three motion lights across the back of the house, which, until recently, had seemed ample. Come morning, he'd make arrangements to have additional security measures taken.

Standing beneath the shade of the oak closest to the house, Alec studied the facade with the wraparound porch. Even if Martinez had opted to get some sleep, there would be no reason to turn off every light in a house that he was only vaguely familiar with.

Alec took the steps quickly and as silently as possible. He slipped the key in the lock and turned it. With a nudge, the door drifted open. Without stepping inside, he scanned the interior. Everything seemed quiet.

The security system's touch pad flashed on the wall. The alarm system was still engaged. Maybe Martinez was just asleep. In another fifteen seconds, when the siren went off, he wouldn't be.

Alec stepped just inside the door and punched in the code. He glanced toward the darkened den, and then the stairs, recalling Jack's suggestion that Martinez was half in love with Katie. Was that where Martinez was? With Katie? The idea left Alec with a hollow feeling in his gut. It had been a lot of years since he'd allowed jealousy to overtake him.

Pushing the door closed, he came face-to-face with a 9 mm automatic held by Martinez.

"I didn't hear you pull up," Martinez said. Even in the dark, the kid looked nervous.

Alec lowered his weapon. "That's because I didn't." He reholstered the Glock and, after closing the door, reset the alarm. "Why no lights?"

"About an hour ago, I was in the kitchen when the motion light out back clicks on. When I look out, there's nothing to see. I don't think anything about it. Then it happens again a few moments later, and again nothing. When it happens a third time, I start to get the feeling that someone's out there playing games."

Usually crime scene officers in cities the size of Deep Water were required to ride patrols as well as work scenes. Because they did, they tended to have better instincts.

"A lot of deer move through here," Alec said.

"Maybe so, but all three of the rocking chairs on the front porch began rocking. A deer didn't do that." Martinez moved into the living room. He stood to one side of the French door, looking out. "I got the feeling somebody was trying to get me out there to investigate."

Alec had followed Martinez into the room. "What about Katie? Does she know what's been going on?"

"No. She went up to bed about two hours ago."

"Is her door locked?"

"Yeah. I checked it after the lights came on the first time."

"But you didn't call for some backup?"

"Because a few motion lights came on and some rocking chairs started rocking?"

Alec tried to control his irritation. Clearly, the kid hadn't wanted to call for backup because he was worried it might damage his image.

"This isn't a two-bit street creep we're dealing with here. This is a criminal capable of outthinking, outmaneuvering the most experienced law enforcement officer. Your job tonight was to keep Katie safe. You should have called for backup."

Martinez remained silent, but Alec could tell that he was pissed. Alec didn't care. Maybe the kid would leave out the testosterone the next time he made a decision.

Alec had followed Martinez to the glass door, but now stepped out in front of the glass. There was a better than even chance that the steps Alec had heard in the brush earlier had belonged to a man. That he'd been within feet of the killer. Perhaps he'd even walked right by him.

But was the killer still out there? Moving through the brush? Watching? Perhaps even gloating that Alec had come that close?

Alec rested his hand on the butt of the Glock and stared into the darkness.

"Man, what are you doing?" Martinez asked. "You're going to get shot, standing there like that."

Alec looked at Martinez. "He was playing head games with you, I just thought I'd give him a little bit of the same."

"I'm not sure which one of you makes me more nervous," Martinez said.

"Both of us should worry you. The UNSUB because if you get in his way, he'll kill you without thinking about it. And me because if you do anything that puts Katie at risk again, I'll make you wish that he got to you first."

Alec headed for the back door. "Wait here. If I'm not back in twenty minutes, call my brother."

Slipping outside, he first checked down by the water. The moon provided enough light to move around, but not enough to do a thorough check for footprints. That would have to wait for morning. And if a small boat or canoe had been utilized to gain entrance it wasn't there now. Alec scanned the narrow moonlit river that was the boundary between his property and the preserve. They'd had little rain in the past two months, so the waterway was more shallow than usual, but a small boat or canoe would still be required to gain access. That or an intruder would have to be willing to do the breast stroke with the alligators.

The only remaining possibility was that the killer had managed to breach the wrought iron security fence that surrounded the rest of the property.

After checking out the area between the front of the house and the road and finding nothing, Alec climbed the front steps. The moonlight that filled the oak hammock leached the color from the leaves and fronds and bark until the landscape resembled a black-and-white photograph.

Whatever the reason for the visit, their guy was now gone. But coming up on the porch had been a big risk for the killer. Why take it? To demonstrate how close he could get?

As Alec turned to go inside, he saw something shiny at his feet. He crouched down to get a better look. It was a necklace.

He stared out into the night once more. He recognized the heart-shaped pendant, encrusted with dark stones. This made the second time he'd seen it today. The first time it had been around Jolie Kennedy's neck.

Alec glanced at the closest French door and saw Martinez standing there watching.

"So that's what he was doing on the porch," Alec said. "You will need to get your camera."

After Martinez had photographed its position on the porch, Alec used the end of a ballpoint pen to pick up the necklace. It swung back and forth like an unsteady pendulum.

Alec carried it into the kitchen and placed it on a clean piece of paper from the pad next to the phone. "It belonged to Jolie."

Martinez, who had been examining the necklace, looked up. "Are you sure?"

Alec nodded. "Any chance of getting prints?"

"I can try fuming it." Occasionally, placing an item in a closed container with superglue revealed prints that hadn't been apparent before, but considering there was little smooth surface on the piece, it was doubtful they'd be successful.

Martinez used the end of the pen to point to what was most likely dried blood on the chain. "Jolie's?"

"Probably." Alec ran a hand roughly through his hair. He was going to have to not only tell Katie about the murder, but also tell her just how close the killer had gotten tonight. How would she react when faced with both at once?

Martinez's voice broke into Alec's line of thought. "How'd it go at Katie's place?"

"About as well as can be expected with an outdoor crime scene and the rain. They brought in a canvas structure and lights, but the scene had already been exposed for more than an hour when they did it."

"You want me to hang out here until morning?" Martinez asked. "Just to be on the safe side?"

"No. He won't be back tonight."

When Martinez headed for the front door, Alec stopped him. "Thanks for staying with her."

Martinez looked at the hand Alec held out. "I didn't do it for you."

"I know," Alec said, his hand still hanging in the air between them. "She makes it easy to care."

Martinez finally took his hand and shook it. "Yes. She does." He immediately reached for the door knob, but didn't turn it. "This is probably none of my business, but has your brother said anything? About the fact that his ass is on the line? That he may lose his job?"

Lose his job? Alec frowned. "What are you talking about?"

"There are a lot of people, including most of the town council, who feel you're bad for Deep Water. They've been putting pressure on the mayor to fire Jack, in hopes that if he's forced to move on, you will, too." Martinez reached for the knob again. "I guess I feel pretty much the same as the town council. That the best thing that could happen to Jack and to this town is for you to leave it."

Alec had sensed Martinez's loyalty to Jack and respected him for it. Like Martinez, Alec would do anything to help Jack. He'd even leave town if that was the answer. Unfortunately, it wasn't. The only chance Jack had of keeping his job now was to see this mess through to the end.

"That's not going to happen," Alec said quietly.

Martinez looked down as if considering his next words. Looking up, he spoke, "Jack said the same thing."

Alec closed and locked the door after Martinez, then prowled into the unfurnished living room to stand at the French doors, watching as the kid climbed into his black sport coupe and drove away.

Moonlight slipped beneath the overhangs, and as the branches of the oaks had on the driveway, the carved bric-a-brac details of the Victorian created intricate designs on the floors.

Staring out, he shoved his hands into the pockets of his slacks. Jack's job was on the line. Brothers were supposed to share those types of details about their lives. But Jack had chosen not to. Just another indication that, in spite of the months rolling past, Alec still hadn't found a way to mend the relationship.

Alec had come to Deep Water to reconnect with his brother, not to mess up his life. No one had been happier than Alec had when Jack had left Atlanta. Jack had worked nearly five years undercover on some of the most dangerous streets in the South. When his cover was blown by an overzealous prosecutor, he'd needed to make a change, and the offer to head up Deep Water's force had seemed the perfect answer.

Alec realized now that he should never have come here. If he hadn't, Katie wouldn't be the target of a brutal killer, Jolie Kennedy would be alive and Jack wouldn't be fighting to keep his job.

But there was no going back. His leaving wouldn't undo any of those things.

His gaze fell on the large oil painting of the two surfers, and Alec crossed to the mantel where he'd placed the painting. She didn't deserve what was happening to her. Any more than his brother did. Maybe Alec wasn't directly to blame for the situations each of them faced, but he was responsible. Somehow, he had to make it right. For both of them.

THE SOUND OF VOICES downstairs woke Katie. She read the digital clock on the nightstand—7:12 a.m. In an attempt to get a fix on who the voices belonged to, she listened for another few moments, and failing that, swung her legs over the edge of the bed.

Once upright, though, she sat there, battling the wooziness. She'd given in and taken a Valium but now wished she hadn't. It had left her feeling as if she couldn't wake up. And she needed to be sharp for the coming conversation with Alec. After their talk in Jack's office yesterday, she was afraid he'd try to send her away. And she was more determined than ever to stick it out. Not just because she wanted her life back, but also because she wanted Alec to get his back.

Katie rubbed her eyes. The cat was still curled on the sheets. He'd insisted on sleeping with her the past two nights, usually near the foot of the bed. Once or twice during the night, though, his loud purr had awakened her. When she'd opened her eyes, he'd been sitting next to her, his staring eyes locked on her face. The first time she'd found it a bit unnerving, but after that, she found it almost comforting. She reached out and ran her hand along the cat's side. Immediately the vibration began.

She'd spoken to her father last night. Her mother had just been released from the hospital. It had been a mild stroke. They were going to rent a small furnished apartment in Sedona for a month or so, until her mother was ready to travel again. Her father had asked when Katie would be able to come out. She'd told him in a week or two. She didn't know what she was going to tell him when a week or two had gone by. Maybe the truth.

Ten minutes later, having dressed in jeans and a black, high-necked sweater, Katie went looking for Alec. Given the raised voices, he wasn't hard to find. Nor was it surprising that neither he nor Jack immediately noticed her presence in the kitchen doorway.

Jack, who was dressed in uniform, dumped his coffee down the drain. "I would have thought what happened yesterday would be enough to convince you how wrong you are."

His back to Katie, Alec faced his brother. Instead of his usual dress slacks and shirt, he had on well-worn jeans that molded to his lean hips and backside, and a faded dark green T-shirt that revealed muscled shoulders.

"It's done just the opposite," Alec said calmly, though there was an edge to his voice that she hadn't heard there often. "He made a mistake last night. He'll make another one soon. Next time, I'll be there when he does."

The mug landed loudly in the bottom of the sink and, scowling, Jack swiveled his head toward his brother. "A mistake? A woman is dead!"

"Don't you think I know that? Jesus. Do you think this is easy for me?"

Dead? The one word had emptied her lungs like a sharp blow to the gut. Who was dead? What were they talking about? Katie felt the last of the Valium-induced muzziness drop away and suddenly wished it hadn't.

The cat brushed against her leg, but kept walking toward his food bowl.

"All I'm saying, Alec, is that it ought to be Katie's decision, made only after she knows everything. Including what went on here last night."

She tried to breathe, but found it difficult. What had gone on here last night? What had happened, and why did Jack seem to think Alec might not tell her?

Jack was the first to see her, a look of uncertainty briefly settling over his features. Seeing his brother's expression, Alec turned as she stepped into the kitchen, his gaze meeting hers without hesitation. But he didn't say anything, and she suspected that he was waiting to see just how much of the conversation she'd overheard.

She took another few steps. Her feet were bare, and the chill of the stone floor climbed through her. "Who's dead?" Her glance skipped from Alec's face to Jack's, before settling on Alec's once more.

Jack moved in behind his brother. "Do you want me to stay for this, Alec?"

"No," he answered grimly. "I'll take care of it."

Looking relieved, Jack picked up the cowboy hat from the counter. "Then I'll go check to see if my men have turned up anything useful."

Katie glanced past Alec and out the window over the sink. Low clouds hung just above the tree line, appearing to sweep in from the direction of the preserve. Half a dozen police officers seemed to be checking out the ground between the house and the trees. Jack's words echoed in her mind yet again, and this time she felt the swelling sense of fear.

Alec waited until the door had closed behind Jack before pulling out one of the tall barstools at the kitchen island. His face was grim. "Perhaps you should sit down."

Instead of moving toward it, she took a step backward. "I'll stand," she said firmly.

Alec took the stool he'd offered her, bracing one foot on the floor and the other on the bottom rung. He obviously hadn't slept much, nor had he taken time to shave.

"What's going on?" she said tightly. "What are all those men out there looking for?"

He glanced down at his hands, which were clasped loosely in front of him, then up at her. "A reporter named Jolie Kennedy was found murdered outside your place last night."

Katie covered her mouth. "Why?" she asked haltingly. "Why...why would he kill her?"

"She was about the same height and build as you, same hair color."

She dragged in a deep breath. He allowed her to make the connection. "He thought it was me." Even as she said it, the color leeched from her face, her heart rocketed up to a hundred and twenty beats per minute.

"Why was she even there?"

"She'd made the connection between your assault and Jill's murder. She wanted to do a story, but I convinced her station manager to hold off. She must have thought if she came up with something more, her manager might change his mind."

He came around the counter, and when she would have turned away, he stopped her. "There's more, Katie."

More? How the hell could there be anything more? Wasn't another woman dead enough?

She lifted her chin and waited, prepared for more bad news.

Alec's eyes seemed to study her for another second. "He also came here. We found Jolie's necklace outside on the porch."

She tried to back away, but Alec wouldn't let her go. He

forced her gaze to meet his. She could see the fatigue, the strain of not just the past week but the past year in his eyes. She'd been living in the nightmare for a matter of days, and it was threatening to eat her alive; she couldn't even begin to imagine what a whole year would be like.

"Now would be a good time to get out, Katie. While you can."

She took a deep breath and let it out slowly. Then took another. And another. Get out, and do what? Run? Spend the rest of her life looking over her shoulder, never knowing if and when it would happen? Afraid to open a door? Afraid to go anywhere near her parents? Afraid. Afraid. Afraid.

And Alec? Let him go on as he was now? Possibly day after month after year? He was a strong man, but even strong men eventually broke.

She didn't want to see that happen to Alec. And she wanted her life back. She wanted to be able to get on a plane and go see her mother.

"Get out? Hell, no! I want to get this sick bastard!"

Chapter Thirteen

Just after midnight, Alec sat in an overstuffed leather chair opposite the door to Katie's room, one foot propped on the ottoman, the Glock and a tall glass of grapefruit juice within easy reach on the small side table.

Katie had gone to bed more than three hours ago. She hadn't been alone when she did. Demon cat had followed her in, bouncing up on the bed and immediately claiming a spot at the foot as if he had every right to be there. Alec didn't know why the sight had irritated him so much. It just did.

Eyes closed, Alec rested his head against the chair cushion. He never slept well after attending an autopsy. Sometimes, like tonight, it was worse than other times.

Most people would have expected Jolie Kennedy's murder to force Katie back into hiding, but it hadn't. Instead, it had made her even more determined.

He had worked with a lot of very talented and brave people who, because of their principles, were willing to put their lives on the line on a daily basis. But not one of them had been any more courageous than the woman sleeping in his guest bedroom.

He knew it was emotionally healthy for him to be having thoughts about another woman—it was a step in the recovery from a loss—but he also knew that the situation they were in clouded emotions. How much of what he was feeling for Katie had to do with guilt? How much of what he saw in her eyes when she looked at him was motivated by a sense that he was her protector, that he alone would keep her safe?

For the past three hundred and sixty-one days, he'd adhered to a daily ritual. He would close his eyes and call up the image of Jill. Tonight, he'd had more trouble with the exercise.

It was some time later, maybe an hour or so, when he heard sounds of movement in her room. The door opened and she stood there, wearing another of his T-shirts, a dark one. The white lettering across the front read: PROPERTY OF THE FBI. Jill had given him it as a birthday present one year, a not-so-subtle reminder that she felt as if the job owned more of him than she did.

The shirt was shorter than some of the others, leaving Katie's long, shapely legs exposed. He curled his fingers into a loose fist, recalling just how smooth and silky her thighs were.

She walked toward him, out of the moonlight and into the shadows where he sat.

His foot hit the ground silently, and he sat up. "Did you need something?"

She rubbed her arms. "I haven't been able to get to sleep. And you don't seem to be planning to…" She glanced down at the cat that had followed her out, and now brushed against her bare legs. "When I was at Martinez's it sometimes helped to play cards. Just to take the edge off." She propped one knee on the ottoman. "I thought maybe, if you were willing, we could try a few hands of poker."

He could think of other, more enjoyable ways to take the

"edge" off. And the only type of poker game that came to mind when he looked at her was the strip variety. It wouldn't take many winning hands before she'd be... And he'd be...

His body tightened at the image of tangled sheets and legs. Alec ran a hand over his face. "Sure." He slipped the Glock into the shoulder holster as he stood. "Why don't you get on some more clothes? I'll meet you in the kitchen."

He'd put on coffee for himself and milk for Katie when the phone rang. Standing next to it, he picked it up before it could ring a second time. His adrenaline was already pumping hard before he spoke a greeting. Middle-of-the-night phone calls never brought good news.

"This is...with the Philadelphia...Department."

Alec could barely make out what was being said because of the amount of background noise. Sirens and shouting and traffic sounds. "This is who?"

"Detective Evans," the man attempted to shout to make himself heard this time. "We have your wife's killer in custody."

These were words Alec had been waiting to hear, but he hadn't expected them to come tonight. Especially not from anyone in Philadelphia.

"Are you sure? You have a confession?"

"No. Not yet. We just put the perp into an ambulance."

"How bad is he?"

"Not good. When he spotted us, he ran. Unfortunately, he forgot to look both ways before crossing King Boulevard and an SUV clocking between forty and forty-five hit him. One leg's busted all to hell, and he's got a head injury. There's a strong probability that the state's going to save some money on this one."

"Do you have a name?"

"David Adams. Mean anything?"

Alec ran the name through his mind. "No."

"He's twenty-eight. Reps for a medical supply company based in Boston, but he has a local address here."

Because it would account for how each of the postcards had been postmarked from a different city and state, traveling sales had been considered as a possible profession for the UNSUB.

"When you talk to his employer, you might want to get a list of where his job has taken him over the past year, and if he has to file an expense report, we might be able to use that—"

"Listen, Alec, as far as federal guys go, you're not too bad, but I do know how to do my job. Right now I'm working to establish a connection to you. With Seth Killian and the FBI's help, of course. I'll call you when I have more."

"Wait. Is there any way to nail down that Adams was out of town last night?"

"Maybe after we question his neighbors. But don't worry. He's our guy. The fact that he was in Philly tonight doesn't mean he wasn't in Deep Water last night. It's a three-hour flight, or a seventeen-hour drive."

What the detective said was all true, but it wasn't enough for Alec. "What about receipts? Anything in his wallet? An airport or gas receipt? Anything that would put him here? Or put him there?"

"Hold on," Evans said. "I've got someone here who wants to talk to you."

"Alec, this is Seth." Alec recognized his good friend's voice, though it was much more tense that usual… "Let me find a quieter spot." Seth and Alec had worked together when Alec had still been with the FBI. They'd been close, closer than brothers, and it had been Seth who had kept Alec sane in those first few weeks following Jill's funeral.

Another few seconds passed, seconds in which Alec tried to picture what was going on there.

Seth's voice broke into Alec's thoughts. "You there?"

"Yeah. How did it happen?"

"Philly PD staked out Jill's grave site and got lucky. David Adams showed up just after ten with a dozen red roses. A few days too early, but that could be because he figured no one would be watching quite yet. It won't be the one year anniversary for another—"

"I know the date," Alec said quietly.

There was a slight pause on the other end. "I know you do."

Alec could hear what Seth left unspoken. That he, too, remembered the date, that Jill had been important to a lot of people.

"Hold on, Alec." Sounds were suddenly muffled as if someone had placed a hand over the phone. Then the noise level returned. "Evans says you're interested in the receipts in Adams's billfold."

"I'm just looking for anything that ties him to Deep Water last night."

"Got an airport receipt for parking that puts him leaving the airport just after one thirty this afternoon. The car had been there two days, so the timing is good for him to have been in Florida."

"But no receipts for hotels or restaurants?"

"Not on him. And we haven't located his car yet. A couple of patrolmen are cruising the streets in the area." Seth paused. "What are you worried about, Alec? That the man who killed Jill isn't the same one who killed the reporter last night?"

"I guess I'm questioning the evidence, and I can't understand why you're not. From the sounds of it, all Philly

PD has is a guy who shows up in a cemetery at night with a dozen red roses. Hell, maybe he was looking for his grandmother's grave and got lost in the dark, ended up standing over the wrong one."

"Adams is the right man. I would stake my career on it."

"How can you be so damn certain? Before DNA comparison comes back, before you question him?"

"Because he was wearing Jill's necklace. And because he had a picture of her in his billfold."

Alec took a deep breath and tried to absorb what his friend had just said. Jill's necklace, the gold dolphin that he'd given her on their honeymoon, had been hanging around David Adams's neck. "What picture?"

"Just a picture," Seth said. "One he took of her that night."

Alec clenched his eyes shut as if that could lock out the image. The ultimate souvenir. A photo of the victim taken in the hours or minutes before death, or sometimes taken afterward, the body carefully posed. He tried to breathe past the tightness in his chest.

"I'm sorry, Alec," Seth said, his voice filled with regret. "I know none of this is easy for you. Or for any of us who knew Jill. Perhaps I should have waited until morning to call, when I'll have better answers for you, but I thought with what you're dealing with down there, you'd want to know as soon as possible."

"You're right." He scrubbed his face. "I needed to know."

"It's over," Seth said, but there was a heaviness in his tone.

"I'll catch a flight tomorrow. As soon as I take care of some things here."

"You might as well wait. At least for a day or two. Even if Adams pulls through, chances are we won't be allowed in right away."

After hanging up the phone, Alec stood staring at it for

several minutes, his hands curled into tight fists, planted on each side of the wall-hung phone. He'd expected to feel relieved, but he didn't. If anything, he felt empty.

Was it because he hadn't been there? Hadn't looked David Adams in the eye? Hadn't held a gun to his head and made him plead for his life?

Alec wasn't a vicious man. He'd seen too much of it in his life to ever believe that violence solved anything. So what was it? Why wasn't he able to feel anything but this numbness? He'd loved his wife. He may not have been a good husband, but he had loved her.

HAVING CHANGED into jeans and a white blouse, Katie walked into the kitchen and found it empty. She scanned the room. Cards rested in the center of the granite island, as did a container of toothpicks. The coffee had finished brewing. And whatever that was on the stove, it was long past the point of no return. But where was Alec?

She turned off the burner beneath what she suspected must have been milk but now resembled dried yellow scum and smelled as appetizing as burnt rubber. After running water into the pan, she left it soaking in the sink.

Admitting that she was suddenly uneasy, she grabbed a knife from the block. Because it was the closest room and the door was open, she stepped into her temporary studio. Instead of the usual smells of oil paints and turpentine, the air carried the scent of orchids, and Katie realized the French doors leading out into the solarium were open.

She moved cautiously through them and into another world—a more exotic one where the smell of wet, dark soil was like a rich perfume.

For some reason—perhaps because the room's glass ceiling magnified it—the moon seemed both brighter and larger and appeared to hang close overhead, filling the cavernous metal and glass structure with light.

Tall palms in oversize pots encircled the room, leaving the center empty but for the two Victorian couches.

Alec sat on the end of one, bathed in moonlight, his head between his hands, his shoulders hunched forward. As she watched, he raked his hands slowly through his hair as if desperately trying to wipe something from his mind.

What had happened? Had the phone call been bad news? Another murder? Katie left the knife on the edge of the plant shelf. God. She couldn't handle much more of this.

Were the horrors ever going to end? Was this going to be what her life was like from now on? This uncertainty? This fear?

The stone floor that acted as a passive solar collector during the day radiated warmth beneath her bare feet, but even that couldn't ease the sharp chill that seemed to climb her spine with each step. She expected him to look up as she approached, but he didn't.

She was only a few feet away when he spoke in an emotionless tone, "I'd like some privacy."

Glancing back the way she had come, she briefly considered doing as he asked. But then what was she going to do? Wait to see if he was willing to talk? Ready to talk? She might very well lose her mind before either of those things happened.

When she didn't move, Alec looked up and seemed to study her with that cool, detached expression of his.

She took another step closer. "Who was that on the phone a few minutes ago?"

"Detective Evans with the Philadelphia police department."

"What did he want?"

"It's over, Katie."

Her eyes narrowed. What was he saying? What was over? "What do you mean?" she asked cautiously.

"They caught Jill's killer," he said and let out a harsh breath. "Tonight. In Philadelphia."

The words both stunned and confused her. "They're sure? There's no possibility of some kind of mistake?"

"No." He shook his head, then looked up at her.

"So that means—"

"That means we can all get on with our lives."

Was it really possible? That just when she'd thought she couldn't cope for another minute, the nightmare was suddenly over? That after all the times she'd been certain she wouldn't, she had survived? She closed her eyes as relief washed over her, loosening the hard knot in her gut. For the first time in days, she managed to really breathe.

She could have her life back, she realized. Could go back to painting. Could do anything she wanted to. Buy a ticket to go see her parents.

But what did she want? Katie looked down at Alec. Why was he so still? Why wasn't he expressing happiness, or relief?

She sat on the second couch, facing him, uncertain what was going through his mind, but realizing that it was something very difficult. And she knew that, even as just a friend, she couldn't leave him alone with whatever it was that he wrestled with.

She started to reach out to touch him, but then pulled her hand back. "Alec?"

"Go to bed, Katie. It's over," he repeated quietly, but with an edge.

"You sound as if you're trying to convince yourself of that."

He let out a ragged breath. "Sometimes, you have a habit of pushing too much." He ground the heels of his hands against his eyes, and then let his fingers dangle between his legs. She could almost see him deciding that it would be easier to tell her.

"Making certain Jill's killer was brought to justice was the last thing I could do for her. Now it's done. She no longer needs me." He tried a wry smile, but even that failed. "That really sounds out there, doesn't it? My wife's been dead for nearly a year, and yet I still talk as if she has needs."

Was he just feeling as if a large part of the reason he got out of bed each morning had suddenly disappeared?

"The dead do have needs." Katie reached out, resting her fingers on his knee this time. "I felt all those things with Karen, too. I remember the week after her death because there were funeral arrangements to make." She smiled sadly. "I recall the trial. The weeks of testimony." She straightened. "But most of all, I remember the terrible moment that came after the verdict was read. Because I realized that it was time to let go. That in most ways, she wasn't part of my future, that she had finally and forever entered the past."

She slipped down on her knees in front of him. They'd been through so much over the past week. She couldn't begin to say that she really knew Alec, but she did know he was a good man, a caring man. And she knew that she was falling in love with him.

He looked at her, his eyes still bleak.

"Time heals, Alec. Sometimes, like now, it's hard to remember that, but it does. You just have to wait for it to happen. Have faith that it will."

Reaching out, he let his fingers drift over her cheekbones, then her lips. "You look so damn fragile, but you're not."

She was a big girl. She knew where they were headed, and she knew she could stop it with a single word. But she wanted it to happen, more than she had wanted anything in recent memory.

She'd been playing it safe all her life. Just over a week ago, a monster had entered her life. But no matter how abhorrent the experience, it had given her something the previous twenty-seven years hadn't. The ability to live in the moment. Not to think about the past or the future. To live as though the present was all that she had.

"No, I'm not fragile," she agreed.

He threaded his hands into her hair and held her gaze as he lowered his lips until they were only an inch from hers. "If you tell me to stop, I will," he said, his voice ragged.

When she didn't say those words, his well-formed male mouth crashed down on hers, emptying her lungs of air and her mind of coherent thought. The heat of it left her light-headed.

Needing something to hold on to, she ran her hands across his chest, enjoying the hard masculine feel of it beneath the T-shirt. He was built lean, like a long-distance runner, but his chest was still broad and well-formed.

When her hands encountered the leather of his shoulder holster, she tried to push it aside. His mouth still on hers, he shrugged out of it.

She immediately trailed her hands over taut abs and felt her own pulse beat even more unsteadily. Needing to feel bare skin, she twisted her fingers into the bottom of his T-shirt.

With a sudden jerk, she freed the shirt from his jeans and peeled it upward. When she could go no further, Alec pulled it over his head and tossed it away.

Still kneeling, her hips trapped between his hard thighs,

she looked at him. In an artist's reverent awareness of his physical perfection, she ran her open palms down the corded muscles of his neck and across his shoulders, her gaze following her hands.

He was beautiful. Deep brown hair, longer at the back. A chiseled mouth, the lower lip slightly more full. Intense, nearly black eyes looking at her with a hunger that made her heart skip a beat, and then race in reaction.

She'd been wanting this, but suddenly wondered if she was really prepared.

"I guess it's my turn," he said with a slow smile. Efficient fingers unbuttoned the first of a dozen small buttons running down her shirt. Nearly losing her balance, Katie rested her open hands on the tops of his thighs. She could feel the heat and the power beneath them.

She wasn't wearing a bra, so when he pushed the shirt aside, there was no more hiding. He ran the backs of his fingertips along her collarbone as his eyes studied her.

"Courageous and beautiful," he murmured, his fingers sliding across her nipples. Instead of stopping there, they continued downward to her jeans where he undid the snap. The zipper rasped in the stillness, the sound seeming to echo somewhere deep inside her.

Picking her up, he carried her backward onto the antique sofa. He tugged off her jeans, then ran his palms upward until he reached the narrow elastic of her panties. Slowly, he pulled them down. Hot hands and cool air—a potent combination that instantly robbed her lungs of oxygen and sent the blood pooling low in her body.

She reached for him, and after shedding the rest of his clothes, he stretched out beside her.

Katie dragged his mouth to hers, opening her own for him with a hunger she'd never experienced. His tongue slid inside, delving, learning, tasting. When she could barely catch her breath, he abandoned her lips. Pushing her hair aside, he kissed the side of her neck, his teeth nibbling. Closing her eyes, she allowed herself to sink into the delicious heat that poured through her as he trailed kisses just beneath her jawline.

As his breath brushed across her breast, white-hot need went through her, and she found herself arching upward, desperate for the feel of his mouth on her. His lips closed over her nipple. Wave after wave of sensation washed through her.

Her abdominal muscles quivered when his hand stroked downward. Even as his tongue flicked across her hardened nipple, he took her intimately with one finger, then with two. Her pelvis rocked upward and he moved inside her.

Her fingers twisted into velvet as she came hard. Instead of stopping, he took her with his mouth, his tongue stroking her into another orgasm even before the first had faded.

And then, when she didn't think she could wait another minute, he covered her body with his.

Moonlight poured over his rock-hard male body. His skin was already slick. His breath may not have been as ragged as her own was, but it wasn't steady, either.

He held her gaze as he slowly pushed into her. She couldn't breathe, couldn't think as he filled her, her body stretching to accommodate him but quickly tightening around him at the delicious drag of flesh against flesh.

She started to close her eyes, but Alec reached out and brushed his fingertips over her mouth. "Don't hide from me, Katie."

He thrust into her fully for the first time, going deeper

and at the same time taking her higher than she ever thought possible. Several more short thrusts had her on the precipice once more. Instead of sending her over the edge, he went suddenly still, and, lifting his hand, smoothed the hair away from her face. His fingers tenderly brushed across her eyelids, flowed across her cheekbone, caressed the line of her parted lips. She could taste them, the heady flavor of their lovemaking. She tried to move, but he held her unmoving beneath him as her feminine muscle continued to pulse around him.

The kiss started out slow and gentle and tender, but quickly turned hungry and raw. He thrust into her again and again. Her hips rocked up as another climax washed over her, this one even more intense. And then, with a ragged groan of release, he throbbed inside her.

SEVERAL HOURS LATER, with dawn only a few hours away and a heavy rain battering the glass roof, Alec pulled on his jeans. He retrieved the Glock from the second sofa. He started to pull his holster over his bare chest, but realized he no longer needed to carry a gun in his home.

After locking the weapon in his desk, he got a glass of water and wandered back into the solarium. The moon had slipped lower, so that it now filtered through the fronds of the potted palms, casting shadows onto the sleeping woman.

When he'd vowed that he wouldn't touch her, he'd told himself that it was because he was protecting her, but the opposite was true. He'd been protecting himself.

Her dark hair lay tousled and tangled from their lovemaking and her lips were parted in sleep.

She was beautiful. But she was so much more than that, too. An amazing woman, really.

His hands curled into fists to keep him from reaching out and touching her. Alec clenched his eyes, torn between doing what he knew to be right and doing what his heart wanted him to do.

But he couldn't hurt her. No matter how much pain it brought him to let her go, he would.

Chapter Fourteen

Katie was awakened by a strange soft and sporadic howling. It took her a moment to realize that it was just the wind catching in the metal skeleton of the solarium.

Muted light filled the space. At first, she assumed the soft dimness was due to an early hour, but then realized the day was simply overcast. It was the first sound sleep she'd had in weeks, so she'd been really out of it.

Propped on one elbow and still groggy, she scooped her dark hair out of her face. The room looked different. Still very beautiful, but not quite as magical as it had been in the moonlight.

She glanced toward the French doors and wondered where Alec was and how long he'd been gone. It was odd how she felt almost abandoned.

As she shifted, her muscles protested even minimal movements. She'd always thought of herself as being in fairly good physical condition, but last night had shown her that when done right, making love was a full contact sport that required both training and stamina.

Katie swung her legs off the side of the couch and sat there. She licked her dry lips. The light-headedness she was feeling was probably due to dehydration. Pulling the blanket with her, she stood. Her clothes were draped over the back of the opposite couch. Or at least most of them were. It took her several minutes to locate and retrieve her panties from partway up one of the palms.

She pulled on the blouse first and buttoned it. As she bent to tug on the jeans, her breasts brushed the cotton cloth, and she realized just how sensitive Alec's lovemaking had left them.

After folding up the blanket, she glanced toward the French doors. She wasn't quite ready to face Alec. Not because she regretted last night, but because she was afraid that he might. She feared that the only reason he'd made love to her was that, after the news, he'd needed to feel close to someone. She had been the only one there for him to turn to.

In an attempt to loosen the growing knot inside her, she took a deep breath and let it out slowly. She'd told herself that she was capable of living in the moment, but was she?

Could she just walk away after what they had shared and not look back?

Would he?

ALEC FOLDED and then threw two dress shirts into the open suitcase.

Without looking up, he sensed Katie standing in the doorway. He tossed the leather shaving kit into the opposite end of the case. He'd planned to wake her before leaving, but had been putting it off.

As if she knew she was being ignored, she stepped into the room.

With no other choice, he lifted his gaze, his features carefully schooled. She leaned just inside the door, her hands braced against the wall behind her, her backside resting on them.

"Sleep well?"

"Sure."

He opened a dresser drawer, briefly fished around for some navy blue socks. As he flipped them in next to the shirts, he glanced in her direction again. This time he had difficulty looking away.

She wore the same jeans and shirt that she'd been wearing last night, and her feet were bare. She had sexy feet. Maybe it was the pale pink of her nails, or the high instep.

And then again, there wasn't much about Katie that he didn't find attractive. From her body to her mind. But right now, with only a queen-size bed between them, it was damned hard to think about her I.Q. Far easier to remember her tight, sleek body, which he'd buried himself in only hours ago, than the well-primed, agile mind.

His body tightened as his resolve to keep his distance slipped. Like a kid standing at a game arcade window with only a quarter in his pocket, he wanted what he shouldn't have. He wanted to tug off the jeans and the prim white shirt, to run his hands over her warm flesh and watch her eyes go dark. To hear the catch in her breath just before she came, to feel those strong feminine muscles tighten around him…

Desperate to derail carnal thoughts, he turned and briefly pretended to scan the nearly empty dresser top. He pushed a hand through his hair. He was forgetting something. Not Katie, but something in the clothing department. He glanced back at the open suitcase, thinking of all the times over the years that he'd done what he was doing now. All the times Jill had stood in the doorway as Katie now did.

She pushed away from the wall. "What's going on, Alec? Shouldn't I be the one packing?"

"Philadelphia called. It looks as if David Adams is going to make it." He grabbed boxers. "I want to be there when he's questioned. Which should be sometime this afternoon." He zipped the suitcase. "I should only be gone a day or two at most." He straightened. "We'll talk when I get back."

The expression on her face told him those weren't the words she'd expected after a night of lovemaking. Unfortunately, they were the only words he had for her right now.

"About last—"

"Listen, Katie. Last night was great. Special. But I don't know where my head is right now. Even if we get a confession, there's still a trial to go through, and after that, there will be appeals."

His mouth tightened. She knew all that, having been down the same road. He just didn't want her expecting anything from him. She deserved better than what he was capable of right now. He'd been a lousy husband the first time around and didn't want to do it poorly a second time. If he ever got involved again, he wanted to be able to put the relationship first. He couldn't do that yet.

She walked toward him, her bare feet soundless on the Persian rug, and, reaching the bed, braced a knee on the edge. "If you're worried about me, you needn't be. I'm a big girl. I'll just collect my things, and..."

He looked at her, his gut twisting with a measure of self-loathing. He should never have let last night happen. "And be on your way?" He finished for her. "Look, Katie, there's no reason for you to go anywhere. I spoke to Martinez. He's planning to come out here to stay with you while I'm gone." He swung the suitcase off the bed and placed it on the floor. For several seconds, their gazes connected, but he couldn't read anything in their dark depths.

Katie backed away. "There's really no reason for him

to. Now that the killer has been caught, I'll be fine." She wandered over to the window and looked out. "If you don't mind, I will stay tonight." She turned to him, the smile on her face forced and fleeting. "It'll give me time to make some arrangements."

He wanted to ask her what kind of arrangements, but didn't. It seemed easier not to. Besides, he expected Jack to come banging on the door at any second.

He picked up the suitcase. "Jack's driving me to the airport, so I'll leave the keys to the SUV on the kitchen counter. And you have my number."

"I think I do," she said, her eyes only meeting his for an instant. But the message was clear enough. She hadn't been referring to a phone number.

In the bright morning light, the last, pale remnants of bruising from the attack were visible. And yet she managed to appear defiant, and he reminded himself that she was a survivor.

But was he? Was he strong enough to walk away from her and not look back? Not regret?

Uncertain, he picked up the suitcase. As he descended the staircase, he looked toward where she stood in his bedroom door. "See you when I get back."

She nodded, but he knew that there was a damned good chance she wouldn't be here.

AN HOUR AND A HALF after Alec had walked out the front door, Katie poured another cup of coffee from the nearly empty carafe, and then wandered into the solarium. She stood in front of the glass wall that overlooked the river and beyond that the preserve. Clouds hung heavy and threatening at the horizon, and the river grasses appeared almost tawny. As she watched, the wind tore across them, briefly flattening them. Shivering as if the gust had climbed her spine, she used her free hand to rub the arm holding the coffee mug.

The branches of the oaks swung around in the stiff breeze. She'd heard some people talking about how unseasonably stormy the first week of November had been this year. Of course, she had nothing to compare it to. Miami had its fair share of inclement weather, but it rarely hung on for more than a day or two.

Though she stared at the landscape, she kept seeing Alec walking away from her. As she replayed his words in her mind, she realized that he'd been trying to tell her that he still wasn't ready to move on. That he had no room in his life for her.

Wrong time, wrong place. That seemed to be a recurring theme in her life of late.

Perhaps it wasn't just Alec's leaving that had her feeling so down and uncertain. Maybe the low barometric pressure and the lack of sunshine were at least partially responsible for her edginess.

She just needed to shake it off.

But she couldn't seem to. It was almost as if some internal monitor had failed to register that she no longer had anything to fear. David Adams was in custody. And as far as what was between her and Alec—well, she'd known the score going in, hadn't she? You couldn't make a person fall in love with you no matter how hard you tried. Even if you were the right woman. They had to be ready. Alec wasn't.

She returned her attention to the landscape. A line of rain showers appeared like a dark curtain in the distance. As she watched, they charged across the preserve. She felt another soft shudder run through her as the first hard drops slapped the glass ceiling.

What she needed was a hot shower. And a plan for getting on with her life. She turned away from the window.

She'd phone her parents again to let them know she'd purchased an airline ticket. By the time Alec returned, she would already be winging west.

Katie rinsed her empty mug and placed it in the top rack of the dishwasher. She'd turned the kitchen's small television on earlier to break the dense silence in the house. When she'd walked into the kitchen, the television had been tuned to a soap opera. Now there seemed to be some type of special news bulletin filling the screen.

A dozen cop cars with emergency lights flashing sat just outside an upscale chain motel's front entrance. As she watched, an ambulance arrived.

There was a cutaway to a reporter. "Senate hopeful Paul Darby was found dead in his Orlando hotel room this morning."

Katie eased up the volume.

"…The police haven't released the cause of death, but foul play is suspected. The politician was perhaps best known as one of Miami's toughest district attorneys, putting criminals like drug czar Benito Binelli and Scott Gardner behind bars. As a strong supporter of environmental issues, Darby has been a very controversial senate contender in many parts of the state where development and growth mean a healthy local economy and a strong job market."

Katie studied the face that flashed on the screen. She'd been leaning against the counter, but now straightened as she finally realized why the name had struck a chord within her all those weeks ago when the first signs had appeared in neighboring yards.

Paul Darby had been the bulldog attorney who had prosecuted her sister's case seven years ago. It had been

Darby who had sent to prison the man behind the wheel of the second car that night.

She had thought about the prosecutor occasionally over the years, recalling the kind way he'd questioned her and the way he'd constantly objected during the cross-examination. He'd been trying to protect her as much as he could. But mostly his words had echoed in her head: Rick Sekorra will pay for your sister's death.

And Sekorra was paying. Not enough, perhaps. He'd have to be six feet under before it would be truly enough. But at least he hadn't walked free. There had been times during the trial when she had been afraid he would.

As she had recounted the events of that night, the jurors had gone still, and tears had collected in the eyes of several, but it had been Paul Darby's closing statement that had the most impact: *Rick Sekorra was a cop, his duty to save lives, and yet on a dark stretch of highway he sentenced two young girls to death. You've heard the evidence. While his wife was struggling with a difficult pregnancy, Rick Sekorra was having a relationship with Karen Carroll, a seventeen-year-old high school senior. And when she threatened to go public, he knew it would end his marriage and his career. So Rick Sekorra decided to take things into his own hands.*

Katie hit the remote, turning off the television.

If she hadn't been depressed enough a few minutes ago, she was now. Paul Darby had been one of the good guys. Who had murdered him and why?

Katie placed the remote on the breakfast bar and headed upstairs. As she passed the front entry table, she saw Alec's phone there. He'd told her to call him if she needed to, and then he'd left his phone behind.

The house held only minimal furniture, but it hadn't felt

really empty until Alec had left. As always, the stairs creaked subtly as she climbed them. The cat streaked ahead of her. He'd been shadowing her for the past hour or more, almost as if he'd taken over Alec's protective duties. Because he seemed to be forever getting in and out of everything, from boxes to empty bathtubs to kitchen cabinets, she'd taken to calling him Houdini.

When the cat reached the top, he sat and waited for her, his tail flicking and his green eyes watchful. He followed her into the bathroom. After closing the door, she stripped off the jeans and the shirt and kicked them in a pile beneath the pedestal sink before turning on the faucet. When she turned around, the cat was still watching her.

"Okay, Houdini. I can handle the bathing thing without your assistance this time."

She picked him up and dumped him back into the hallway. Immediately, a paw shot from beneath the door. She watched for several seconds as the cat used first the right paw and then the left, all the while crying. It was almost like having a toddler tugging on a locked door while you tried to steal two minutes to yourself.

"Go find a mouse or whatever it is you do around here to earn your keep."

Suddenly, as if he'd understood his orders, the antics stopped. Katie grabbed a towel from the pine armoire and placed it within easy reach of the tub, then stripped off her panties and tossed them with her other clothes.

She waited until the water was the right temperature before pulling the curtain surround from both sides, and flicking the diverter up. Water poured out of the large showerhead almost like a summer downpour.

She stepped in over the high side, not an easy task with the way her muscles ached. As the warm water poured over her, heat seeped in by slow degrees. After adjusting the shower head to a massage setting, she dropped her head forward to luxuriate in the way the pounding water loosened the tense muscles of her upper back. The curtain billowed and shifted in the warm air generated by the water like a half-inflated hot-air balloon eager to float away.

For the longest time, she just stood beneath the water, then, when she could feel it starting to cool down, she reached for the soap and the washcloth.

As she ran it across her abdomen, the curtain suddenly plastered itself to her right hip and buttock. Katie pushed out on the material, and as she did so, a strong current of cold air leaked through where the curtains met. She turned and adjusted them to be sure water wouldn't escape.

The bathroom door creaked softly.

Her eyes narrowed. Had she failed to shut it? No. She distinctly recalled making certain the latch caught so that Houdini wouldn't be able to push it open. It was an old house, though, and after only a few days, she didn't know all of its quirks.

"Is that you, Houdini?"

She was already reaching for the faucet when the light from the room's one window suddenly dimmed, someone much larger than a cat having just walked in front of it.

Chapter Fifteen

Having already reclaimed his carry-on, Alec maneuvered past those who were still grabbing their belongings from the plane's overhead luggage compartments.

When he'd phoned this morning, he'd managed to secure the last seat on this flight, but that had meant the past few hours in an aisle seat next to the restroom, and with other passengers standing over him as they waited their turn.

The pilot had attempted to go around the rough weather, but the flight had still been a rough one. More than once, he'd nearly ended up with a fellow passenger in his lap when they lost their balance while standing in line.

As he walked up the aisle, Alec glanced down at the coffee stain that covered his shirt. He'd have to stop somewhere on his way out of the airport and change it.

Throughout the morning, his mind, which should have been on the coming interview with David Adams, had been on Katie. He dragged in a deep breath. Usually, he had no problem compartmentalizing, keeping his thoughts and energies firmly focused on whatever task lay ahead. He'd been known to filter out almost anything and anyone. But not Katie. He tried to tell himself that it was because they'd been with each other 24/7, but the truth was, even before two weeks ago, even before they'd spent any real time together, when the only relationship between them had been that of waitress and customer, she had lingered at the back of his mind.

A heavy, staying hand dropped on his shoulder from behind and Alec swung around abruptly, coming face-to-face with Seth Killian. Several inches shorter than Alec, Seth had nearly black hair that he kept trimmed to the Bureau's specifications. Like Alec, Seth was a runner. Mainly because the only pieces of required equipment were a pair of running shoes and a road or trail, which made it easy to stick to a regimen when out in the field.

They'd been hired and gone through training at the same time. Unlike Alec, who had been recruited while still at the Citadel, Seth had done a stint in the marines before applying to the Bureau. After training, they'd received different assignments, Alec drawing Philadelphia and Seth Minneapolis. It hadn't been until three years ago that they'd both ended up in the same field office.

Usually Seth wore an easy grin, but not now. If anything, Seth looked worried.

They'd arranged to meet outside the hospital, so Alec's gut instantly tightened. Had something gone wrong? Seth had assured him that David Adams's condition had improved enough that the doctor was willing to let them question him.

Alec shifted the bag to his left hand. "Let me guess. The lawyer has pressured the attending physician to keep us out?"

"No. In fact, Detective Evans is in questioning David Adams now."

Alec's fingers tightened on the bag's handle. He cursed aloud and succinctly, something he rarely did. "He knew I wanted to go over strategy before anyone talked to—"

Seth grabbed Alec by the upper arm and turned him back toward the gate area. "David Adams is the least of our problems right now."

"What are you talking about?"

Seth ignored the question. "I have us booked on a flight out of here in six minutes. If we make a run for it, we might just make it."

"A flight where?"

"Daytona," Seth said, his face was tight with concern.

"What's that? About an hour from Deep Water?"

"Less than that." Alec barely missed running over a little girl as he tried to keep up with Seth. "But what in the hell is going on? Why am I getting back on a plane?"

Several planes must have unloaded at nearly the same time, because the walkway became even more congested.

Seth dodged a woman who had stopped to reposition her baggage. "I just got off the phone with David Adams's boss. David Adams was attending a conference in Oregon when the Deep Water assault took place."

"What?" Dread pooled in Alec's gut. "Any chance he checked in and then skipped? Those things are pretty un-structured. People coming and going all the time, no one keeping track."

"His boss says no. He made the trip with Adams and claims he sat beside him from eight to five all three days and had dinner with him each night."

"And two nights ago?" Alec asked, but he already knew what Seth was going to tell him.

"On a plane back from Las Vegas. I checked with the airlines. He was in seat 26A. The plane landed in Philly just after ten that night."

So David Adams hadn't assaulted Katie or murdered Jolie Kennedy. But he had been wearing Jill's necklace, was carrying a photo of her taken the night of her death and had visited the grave site.

He nearly slammed into a man who stopped suddenly in front of him and earned a sour look that he chose to ignore. "Then it's a damn copycat," Alec said between clenched teeth. He scanned the concourse ahead. He'd managed to leave his cell phone behind at the house this morning. "I need a phone."

"If you're worried about the girl, I called your brother on my way over. He's sending someone named Martinez out to your place until we can get there."

Alec felt the adrenaline kicking in as he thought about the timing, about the fact that he'd left Katie unprotected. Exposed. And about their last conversation. Why couldn't he ever seem to get it right?

He'd been scared several times during his career, but never more so than he was at that moment. He tried telling himself that as long as she stayed in the house and kept the alarm system on she would be relatively safe. But he didn't believe it.

Alec glanced at his watch. She'd been alone for more than five hours now. She'd talked about making some plans. Had any of them taken her away from the house? What if she wasn't there when Martinez arrived? What if she'd gone shopping? She didn't have a cell phone. Was there any possibility that she'd taken his, though?

Alec held out his hand. "Give me your cell phone."

Seth passed it to him. Alec dialed his cell number, reached voice mail. Then he tried his brother's cell number. When it went to voice mail, too, he disconnected and tried the Deep Water police station. He was put on hold before he could say half a syllable.

Seth grabbed him by the arm and dragged him through

the crowd toward gate ninety-two—the gate Alec had just left. "This is us."

The door to the gateway was swinging closed as Seth placed the tickets on the counter. "You need to hold that door," he ordered the young male airline employee at the counter.

"The flight's full, sir."

"Then you'll have to ask two people to give up their seats, because we have to be on that plane." He flashed his badge.

Alec saw the hesitation in the man's eyes, and then the sudden realization that he was going to have to hold the flight until two of the passengers who were already aboard agreed to disembark. Turning, the young man picked up the phone and made the call.

Alec managed to get through to Deep Water Police as two passengers, an older couple, emerged from the gateway. He nodded as they passed, and Seth stopped to tell them just how much he appreciated their willingness to cooperate.

A woman's voice brought his attention back to the phone he held. "Deep Water Police."

"This is Alec Blade. I need to talk to my brother."

"Let me see if I can locate him." He was put on hold again.

Looking up, he saw Seth motioning him. Realizing that he couldn't wait any longer, he disconnected and jogged after Seth. He'd have to use an air phone.

The curious stares of other passengers followed them both as they took their seats in first class. Within seconds, the 757 was backing away from the gate. Alec closed his eyes as the plane taxied out for takeoff. In his head, he kept seeing Katie standing framed in his bedroom door. At the time, he'd wondered if it was the last time he would see her.

Now he wondered if it would be the last time he would see her alive.

BOTH MEN WAITED until they were in the air before resuming their conversation.

Alec grimaced. "Early on, I looked at the possibility of a copycat crime, but ruled it out. What in the hell didn't I see that I should have?" He had considered the possibility of a copycat—though perhaps not for very long. The crime scene and the evidence had pointed so convincingly to the same man who had killed Jill.

"Nothing," Seth said. "I examined the same photos, the same evidence as you did, and came to the same conclusion. That both had been done by the same man."

But how was that possible? What was he still not seeing?

"To duplicate the scene in Deep Water would take first-hand knowledge of the Philadelphia scene. Any possibility that David Adams picked up a partner?"

"That's one of the questions Detective Evans is undoubtedly asking Adams right about now. But unfortunately, that's not the only possibility." Seth's expression turned more grim. "Evans called just after I talked to Jack. Part of Jill's file—some photos and a copy of the crime scene technician's notes—is missing."

Alec rubbed his eyes. A copy of notes made by the CST was missing? What next?

"So if Adams isn't working with an partner, whoever our UNSUB is, he knows his way around not only a crime scene, but a police department. Well enough to walk in and help himself to part of a file without anyone noticing."

"It would explain your crime scene." Seth looked up and nodded at the hostess as she wheeled the beverage cart to the front of the plane.

Seth was right. It would explain it, but getting in and out of a police station wasn't easy. And that was if you knew where and what to look for. But the missing notes and photos couldn't be just a coincidence. The details of the two scenes had been too accurate to have been guessed at.

"You said it was the CST's original field notes that were missing and not the report?"

"Just the notes," Seth said. "The report was still there."

Alec grabbed his case from the overhead compartment. From the outside pocket, he collected the thick file. It had grown steadily over the past eleven months and contained everything pertinent to the investigation. In hopes of an early resolution to the murder investigation—his plate full with a dozen more open cases—Evans had been more than willing to share. At least he had been once he'd ruled out Alec as a possible suspect.

Alec found it ironic that his alibi eleven months ago and David Adams's alibi six days ago had been the same—that there had been thousands of feet of air beneath them when the crimes had occurred.

He dropped back into the seat, flipped the tray-table down. He sorted through paperwork for several seconds before finding a copy of the CST's field notes.

Cursing beneath his breath, he placed the folder next to him. "That's what I was seeing, but couldn't put my finger on. In the initial notes, the tech lists the brand of box cutter, the size and number of candles and the fact that they were cheap ones carried by most discount stores. All those things match perfectly with what was used at Katie's."

"What about the surgical tubing?"

Alec looked at Seth. "Just the diameter is given. The manufacturer was in only the final report."

Seth's mouth flattened. "And that's the reason the tubing didn't match. It wasn't because his source changed suppliers. It was because he didn't know what tubing had been used, so he went with the most common brand."

"And guessed wrong." Alec looked toward the front of the plane. "It would take someone who works in law enforcement, or at least someone with a police background, to have so precisely pulled off that crime scene. Everything was just too well done to be someone off the street."

Alec glanced down at the report, then at the photo of Katie's bedroom. He was still missing something here. Some vital connection that he still wasn't making. Why would a cop come after him? True, he had pissed off his fair share of them over the years, but to use a young woman to exact revenge on a fellow law officer…that was really pushing the limits of believability.

But what…Alec lowered the photo, his gut already twisting as he looked over at Seth. "I've been basing everything on the belief that I am the target, but what if I'm not? What if Katie is the target?"

"Considering the crime scene, isn't that a stretch?"

"Either a stretch or genius." Alec seemed to study the photo, but in his mind, he went back to that night. Katie had said her attacker had called her Katydid—a name her sister had given her—and that no one but the ex-boyfriend had known it. Even though they'd never been able to pinpoint how her attacker had come up with the nickname, Alec had assumed it had been on the back of a photo. But what if that wasn't the case?

Alec frowned. "For argument sake, let's say it is Katie. Someone shows up here with the intention of harming her, but doesn't want to be implicated. He somehow recognizes me, or perhaps the local rumor mill gives him enough to get him thinking." Alec glanced at the photo again. "He does his homework, and then does even more of it when he walks into a police department and strolls out with what he thinks is a blueprint. Which leaves only the implementation."

"So who would want the girl dead?" Seth asked. "What cop—"

Alec reached for the air phone, then, holding it to his ear, tugged a credit card out of his billfold. It took several minutes for the call to go through and for Alec to get patched in to Jack.

"Jack—"

Jack cut him off. "Katie's missing. I'm at your place now and it looks as if there's been a struggle in the upstairs bath."

Alec closed his eyes against the sharp pain that cleaved his chest wide open. It was his fault. He'd allowed himself to get tunnel vision. And because he had, Katie was in danger.

"Any blood?"

"No. At least no obvious—" Jack suddenly broke off. "Damn it, Martinez, catch that cat. What in the…what is wrong with him?"

Demon cat let out a long, lethal-sounding growl.

"Forget the damn cat. Any idea how long he's had her?"

"A couple of hours maybe. Maybe less, but there's no way to pinpoint it right now."

Alec took a deep breath. He needed to stay focused. Now more than ever. "I need you to pull a record on an inmate at the South Florida Correctional Facility. On a Rick Sekorra." Alec spelled the name.

"What am I looking for?"

"He went in for vehicular homicide. I need to know if he's still there, and if not, a current address for him."

"What's the connection to you?"

"None. The connection is to Katie. He's responsible for the death of her twin sister. And he was a cop."

Chapter Sixteen

Katie fought the heavy nausea climbing her throat and the pounding pain in her head. Intense sunshine heated her face. Where was she? At the beach? If she was at the beach, why couldn't she hear waves? Or the familiar sounds of seagulls and blaring music? And what of the clean scent of sand and salt water?

Even as she tried to open her eyes, a heavy drowsiness sucked her back down into a warm, black hole. She was tempted to let it, but knew she shouldn't.

But why shouldn't she give in? Let her body and mind backslide into the waiting abyss? Into the waiting tranquility?

Dream. That was what it was. She was just dreaming and was too tired to rouse herself to wakefulness.

Tired from what? Had she gone to the beach? Drunk too many rum drinks? Was that why her head hurt?

No. That wasn't it. But something had happened. She couldn't remember what, but knew that she needed to open her eyes and face whatever it was. Alec's face, tight with passion, lingered in the darkness with her. She tried to lick her dry lips, but couldn't. Something was over her mouth. But what?

Then an odor intruded. A woodsy mustiness that she couldn't place.

A memory speared across her sluggish mind. A shower curtain being ripped back, a man standing there. Katie felt her body jerk once, twice, involuntary movements brought on by the man's face.

Rick Sekorra's face.

Even as the image faded, she could feel his hot breath brush her ear. "Katydid. You need to wake up. It's time to play."

She kept her eyes closed, trying to clear her mind even more.

"Katydid, open your eyes," he whispered. Then louder, "I'm not going to ask again."

She forced her eyes open, but immediately squinted against the sudden pain caused by the blinding light. What she'd thought was sunlight was nothing more than a strong utility lamp clamped to the metal headboard of the narrow bed. She rolled her head away from the man leaning over her. Tasting bile at the back of her throat, she swallowed. If she got sick now, she'd choke.

Though she already knew what she would find, she focused on the binding that lashed her left wrist—and presumably her other wrist and ankles—to the metal headboard and footboard.

Surgical tubing.

The effects of what he had given her were fading, but were just as quickly being replaced by a numbing fear. She was going to die. Panic clawed its way through her, tearing at her as if it were a wild animal trapped inside a canvas sack. Tears welled up hot and fast, immediately clogging her throat. She tried to move more than her head, but realized she couldn't. It was as if her arms and legs were glued to the bare mattress.

He grabbed her chin and forced her to look at him. His eyes were such a pale brown that they looked nearly amber. She remembered them, she realized. She would have known him by those eyes alone.

The night of the accident came screaming back. Those cold snake eyes staring in at her as she sat trapped by her seat belt.

The hair was different, though. His head was clean shaven now, as were his powerful chest and arms.

His face was scratched up, as if some animal…

Alec's cat. The cat had attacked him as he tried to slide the needle into her arm that first time.

But it was the locket swinging from his neck like a pendulum that she couldn't seem to look away from. The one he'd taken the night he attacked her, the one with a photo inside of her sister.

Sekorra squatted down next to the cot, so that he was even with her. He ran a finger slowly from the point of her chin down her throat. When he reached the first button of her blouse, he undid it. "Were you hoping I'd rot in prison, or maybe find God and be willing to turn the other cheek?" He undid the next two, pushed aside the material. Katie clenched her eyes. Everything inside her began shutting down. She wouldn't let him see her fear. No matter what it took, she wouldn't give him the satisfaction of seeing just how frightened she was.

Her eyes flew open, and she tried to jerk away when he brushed back a section of hair that had fallen forward onto her face. He chuckled and leaned closer. "Or maybe you didn't think about me at all. Is that it?" He reached up and flicked off the lamp. "Think about this, Katydid. Think about what it's going to feel like to die."

He closed the door after him, leaving her alone in the pitch-black room. The first hard sob racked her. She tried to move again, but couldn't. What had he given her? How long before the effects wore off, before she could have any hope of fighting for her life?

IT TOOK THREE HOURS, but finally Alec and Seth were back in Deep Water. The two men sprinted through the front doors of Deep Water's police department. And down the hall to Jack's office.

From the moment they'd left the Daytona airport, they'd hit nothing but traffic. He'd spoken to Jack less than half an hour ago, and they'd agreed to meet in his office.

Jack stood next to his desk. His hair was disheveled, as if he'd been shoving his hand through it repeatedly for the past few hours. Martinez and another young officer were reviewing some typed pages.

"Did you get it?" Alec asked his brother.

Jack handed him a photo.

Alec instantly recognized the face. The deep-set pale brown eyes that appeared to be tucked in beneath a pronounced forehead. A blunt nose, squared at the end. Clean-shaven head.

It was the man from the political rally. The one who had stopped Paul Darby's attacker two days ago.

"I see you remember him. He was paroled just over a month ago. And we're fairly certain that Katie wasn't his only target."

Unfolding the *Deep Water Times Union,* Jack laid it in front of Alec.

Politician Found Murdered In Hotel Room

Alec met his brother's eyes. "He stopped someone else from killing Darby because he wanted the pleasure of doing it himself."

"The rally wasn't the only time your paths crossed. You actually had Sekorra in one of the National Academy classes. So it's not surprising he would recognize you." Alec had taught a behavioral science course at Quantico for state and local law enforcement personnel from around the country.

Alec tossed down the paper. "You took his statement?"

Jack handed Alec the report that one of his officers had taken several days earlier. "He's been using the name Richard Sexton. The address is bound to be fake, but—"

Alec looked up, realizing they might have just gotten their first break. "Maybe not. Everything he's done up until this point has shown a strong degree of arrogance. Because he thinks Jill's killer is still out there, Sekorra sees himself as invisible and invincible. He has no idea that we're on to him. He has to make Katie's…" Alec's jaw hardened. "He's got to make it look as if Jill's killer is responsible."

Martinez, who had stood silently by, leaned down until his gaze was level with Alec's. "What happens if he learns David Adams has been apprehended?"

Seth, who had picked up the photo seconds earlier, tossed it back down on the desk. "Then he kills her and dumps the body where he hopes it will never be found."

KATIE DIDN'T KNOW how long she'd been lying there, listening intently for any sound, but it felt like hours. For at least the past thirty minutes or so, she'd been able to move her hands and legs, but had quickly discovered that even the slightest tug tightened the tubing around her wrists and ankles, cutting off circulation.

Where was she? Where had he taken her?

And what was he waiting for?

Her head hurt, but the fuzziness had receded enough that she could think a bit more clearly now.

He'd killed Darby. He'd bragged about it as he slid the needle into her arm. She tried to swallow, but her throat just tightened with unshed tears. Did anyone even know she was missing? And why hadn't he killed her back at Alec's house when he'd had the chance?

The pain above her right eye expanded. Her breathing turned shallow and fast as she fought the burning and aching sensation. The fingers of her left hand already tingled from lack of blood flow.

She glanced toward the door. The room's only light came in beneath it. The floor was bare concrete, or maybe terrazzo, the one window covered over with plywood. Even if she could get herself free, she'd have to get past Sekorra.

Trapped there in the dark, crime scene photos strobed across her mind. Jill's body tied to a bed, the sheet beneath dark with blood. The box cutter resting on the nightstand.

In an effort to close down those images, she forced herself to think about her parents, about the airline ticket she'd bought. She'd never seen the Grand Canyon. Had never been west of the Mississippi. There were a lot of things she hadn't done in her life. She'd always thought there would be more time. To travel. To find and marry the right man. With that thought, she saw Alec smiling at her, his dark eyes warm. Then a second image followed, of Alec again, but this time his features were drawn in concentration as he'd looked up at her, his tongue dipping into her navel briefly before moving lower....

In Alec's arms, she had felt alive for the first time in her life. Alive and safe and free.

It couldn't end now. Not like this. Before she'd truly lived. Before she'd truly loved.

"HOW DO YOU WANT to handle things?" Jack asked Alec as they both pulled on soft body armor.

"We go in hard and fast. Our best hope is to get to her before he moves her. Once he does, it becomes a crapshoot. Though if I had to guess, I'd say he'll take her back to the bungalow."

Trying to stay focused on what lay ahead of them, and not the woman they were going after, Alec tugged on the shoulder holster over the armor. "He won't be looking for us. He still believes himself to be invisible. It's a face card, but it hardly stacks the deck in our favor."

"Do you really think there's an outside chance he hasn't harmed her yet?"

"He could have done it at my place and didn't."

Jack fastened the duty belt around his waist. "Maybe he was worried someone would show up."

Alec slipped a magazine into the Glock, then glanced up again, his expression grim. "Perhaps he's not as comfortable with killing as he thought."

If Sekorra had harmed Katie, Alec was going to take him apart. Nothing would be able to stop him. Not even Jack.

"Tell that to Darby," Jack said bluntly. He had bent down to shove the small revolver into the ankle holster.

"Killing a man by injecting him with Valium, then sliding a couple of rattlesnakes in bed with him isn't quite the same as slicing open a woman while she's still alive. Maybe he doesn't quite have the stomach for it, but he knows that taking any type of shortcut will be a dead giveaway."

Swinging back around, the assault riffle he'd picked up from the rack in his hands, Alec leveled his gaze on his brother. "Are you about ready?"

Jack straightened. "We'll get him."

Wordlessly, he grabbed half a dozen magazines for the assault weapon and rejoined Martinez and the two officers in the other room.

Jack had chosen two young recruits to round out the team. Alec didn't question his brother's decision. Jack knew his men. But Alec wondered how they were going to handle themselves in the next few hours.

The tall redhead had taken some SWAT training. The other, a short Rambo look-alike, had the best time and scores on the gun range. But they weren't going to be running drills or punching holes in paper today. Today they'd both be losing their virginity.

Alec walked to the window overlooking the back parking lot. Was he kidding himself about the possibility that Katie was still alive? He wasn't infallible. And Rick Sekorra wasn't your typical offender. He'd seen the system from the inside, knew how law enforcement worked, how law officers thought. He'd attended courses that Alec had taught on profiling and on crime scenes. He would have learned more by his firsthand observation.

If anything, Alec was the one at a disadvantage.

In an effort to control his nerves, he shoved his hands into his pocket. He knew how important preparation was, but he was having a hard time coping with even the smallest of delays. Because this time, the stakes were so high.

For the first time, he allowed himself to put a name to

it. To admit to himself, if not to anyone else. He loved her. He had fallen in love with Katie the moment she had walked through his front door. Beautiful and defiant. Intelligent. A woman strong enough to stand up to a man and strong enough to stand beside him. It was that very strength that he was counting on to keep her alive until he could get to her. Until he put Sekorra into a well-earned body bag.

Hearing someone enter the room, Alec turned.

Seth folded his cell phone. "That was Detective Evans. He'll continue to keep David Adams's arrest out of the media until he hears from us." Seth shoved the cellular phone into his pocket. "And we finally have the connection between you and Adams. His mother dated Dick Bartow for several years."

Alec knew the name. Bartow had brutally raped and murdered five women in Cincinnati back in the late nineties. Alec had been called in to provide a profile, and it had been his testimony that had put Bartow on death row. Bartow had died there, but not at the hands of the state. Cancer had taken him.

Seth wandered over and stood beside Alec, both men looking out the window. "Evidently, Adams considered him a father figure."

All Alec could think about was the waste of life. Of David Adams's life and Jill's life—and perhaps most of all, the life of the unborn child Jill had been carrying. His child. And all because he'd done his job.

Jack came in, his officers right behind him. "Cars are out back."

They climbed into a beat-up Ford Taurus and a 1991 Chevy Blazer that was so covered in mud and scrapes that it was difficult to tell the paint color. Where they were headed, even an unmarked police vehicle would stand out.

The address Sekorra had given on the report wasn't far

from the springs and down an unpaved road. The homes in the area were a mixture of squat cement block structures or older trailers. Instead of lawns, there were cars on blocks and dogs tied up, their only shelter a rusted fifty-five gallon drum. It was the kind of area where neighbors kept to themselves, where you expected to find illegal migrant workers or meth labs. And Alec knew it was for that reason that Sekorra had chosen it. No one would bother him. And if they noticed anything unusual, the last thing they'd do was call the cops.

Sekorra's frame house sat back from a dirt track that was nearly overgrown with weeds. A chain stretched across the entrance with a rusted No Trespassing sign hanging from it. They left the two cars out of sight and hiked in.

As dusk deepened, a slow, steady drizzle began to fall.

Alec motioned for Jack to work his way around back. Martinez was to wait outside while Alec and the officer with SWAT training went in. The second young cop would wait with Martinez. As they were positioning themselves, a light came on inside.

Seeing it as a fairly reliable indication of Sekorra's position in the house, Alec moved in, keeping low to the ground. Adrenaline screamed through his veins, and his chest was tight with it. The night was cool, the ground muddy from recent rains.

Alec kicked in the door. "Police!"

SEKORRA LEANED IN and, picking her up out of the trunk, slung her over his shoulder. Blood rushed downward into her head, and everything seemed to spin as he swung back after closing the trunk lid. She was wearing a man's T-shirt, but nothing beneath it.

He was going to kill her. Clenching her eyes, she silently dragged in as much air as she could.

Don't panic. Stay limp.

But how? Panic sizzled through her veins, the instinct to fight for life nearly impossible to deny. And her muscles screamed for freedom. The zip ties around her wrists bit into the already bruised flesh. Her hands felt nearly as numb as her head.

Somehow, she managed to control herself. Hanging over his shoulder, she couldn't tell where he was taking her, but they seemed to be cutting through a small hammock of oaks. Tree frogs filled the night with their endless chigg…chigg…chiggering. The sound suddenly seemed to be mocking. Sinister. As if they were in collaboration with the monster who carried her.

She'd been wrong. She shouldn't have forced Alec's hand. How arrogant it had been to think she could outwit a maniac. And so stupid. Alec would blame himself. See it as his failure. But it wasn't. Oh, Alec! She wished she could see him one more time, if only to tell him that he wasn't to blame.

He'd done everything he could to keep her safe. He'd been right. Running wouldn't have changed anything. Sekorra would have followed. But she wasn't going to get a chance to say any of those things. Just as she wasn't going to get the opportunity to tell him that she loved him…had loved him from nearly the first moment he'd looked up at her in the diner, as she waited to take his order.

How simple things had been then.

She should have told him this morning, when she'd had the chance. But she'd been afraid of the words. She hadn't wanted to risk anything, especially her heart. But life was nothing but risks and dreams—some of which, if you were lucky, actually came true. She'd recognized that too late.

Sekorra stopped and, rotating his upper body right and then left, seemed to be scanning the way they'd just come. As if he worried about being followed.

Cautiously lifting her head, she got her first look at where they headed.

Oh, God, no… Any place but here. It was too cruel. Alec had been hurt enough. If he found another bloody body in his own bed, laid out carefully for him, like a gift from hell…

Sekorra used a key to open the front door. Where had he gotten it? And why wasn't the alarm going off?

Once inside, he hesitated. "Honey, I'm home!"

The sarcastic words echoed through the house. When they had nearly died away without any answer, he shifted her weight higher on his shoulder. *Don't tighten up. He'll feel it if you do.* She closed her eyes.

Hold steady. She could hear her father telling Karen to hold the small fishing boat steady. Oh, Karen… This man… this monster…was he really going to kill them both? And then, she felt her heart buck. Did he intend to kill her parents next?

Sekorra climbed upward into the darkness, the combination of his weight and of Katie's making the treads groan beneath him. At the landing, he hesitated again, looking up, and then back down the way he had come. Through the landing window, she could just make out the moon beginning to rise. A deep orange that seemed to sit among the branches of the distant trees. A blood moon.

With a grunt, he dropped her on Alec's bed. Even with her eyes closed, she could feel that ugly face and those amber eyes staring down at her.

Or was he just staring? Perhaps he was getting ready. Pulling out his weapon, deciding where to begin. Her facial muscles stiffened. The urge to see, to know, to be prepared, was nearly impossible to ignore.

He slapped her across the left cheek. "Wake up, bitch!"

Her head snapped away from the blow. Sharp shards of pain exploded through her cheekbone. Duct tape muffled her grunt of pain. Stinging tears blurred her vision.

She rolled her head so she could look up at him.

Smiling, he grabbed her chin and stroked it. "I want your eyes wide-open. I want you to see everything I'm going to do to you."

He shrugged out of his shirt. "I've waited a long time for this." Folding it, he placed it on the corner of the dresser. In the dim illumination that spilled in from the hall fixture, his chest appeared pasty, but massive, with bulging muscles and the defined *cut* of a jail yard bodybuilder.

How could she possibly hope to overpower him? Without a weapon?

But she had to try. She refused to simply lie here and die.

Katie moved as subtly as she could, and, in halting, wriggling inches, she made it to the edge of the mattress closest to the door, when Sekorra noticed. Still opening drawers as if he were looking for something, he smiled at her.

"Katydid. You should save some of that energy. You're going to need it when we start. I'll want you to writhe for me then. When I can watch and enjoy."

After pulling the drapes closed, he prowled around the room some more before coming back to where she lay. He turned on the bedside lamp and then squatted next to the side of the bed. Reaching out, he ran a thick finger across her black and blue cheek, smoothing back a section of hair that was caught on it, his fingers gentle.

She refused to look at him.

Like a cat, intent of torturing its prey, he continued to brush his finger over her face. "You know what I want more than anything?" he asked. He reached down between his legs. "What's guaranteed to give me a real hard-on?"

He leaned in closer still. "Besides getting between those firm thighs of yours?" He leaned down and licked her cheek. "I've been saving up, Katydid. Seven long years without." He reached down and rubbed himself again. His eyes glazed over. "Karen liked it hot and raunchy." He opened Katie's blouse and ran his hand over bare skin. "It'll almost be like doing it with a dead woman.

"But to make it perfect…" He ripped the duct tape off her mouth. "I'm going to need to hear you scream."

He dug a box cutter from his pocket. Flicking the short but lethal blade from the handle, he held it up for her to see.

"Nothing fancy," he said, tilting it in the lamplight so that they both could admire it. "And yet strangely effective. In fact, it has some real advantages. No chance of getting carried away and going too deep, too soon. Ending the fun even before it's begun."

Panic broke free inside her. She was breathing too fast, but she couldn't seem to slow it. Don't hyperventilate. If she passed out now, she might not ever wake up. But no, that wasn't really true. Sekorra wouldn't let her die quickly, unconscious. He wanted her to suffer. He planned to enjoy her pain.

Her heart slammed against her ribs. She had to find some way… For Alec. For her parents. For herself. She wanted so much to live.

With a deliberate sawing motion, Sekorra hacked off her jeans by slitting them from ankle to hip. She could feel the trembling start deep inside her, heavy, involuntary tremors of primal fear.

He retracted the blade with a satisfied snap.

"Before I'm done with you," he said, "You will beg me to kill you." He trailed his fingers up her leg and across her belly. "And I always give ladies what they want. Karen could have told you that."

She couldn't control the way her shoulders jerked and her lungs deflated.

An hour ago, it would have been enough just to escape him. Not now.

Now she hated as he did.

Hated enough to kill.

Tears welled up in he eyes, not just of fear, but also of determination. He was stronger than she was, but he wasn't any more resolved. And perhaps he had a weakness, after all. Perhaps he was a little too confident. He expected her to go meekly to her death, paralyzed by fear. And she wouldn't. If she didn't survive, at least she would force him into killing her quickly. He'd never see her cower and beg. She'd cheat him of that, at least.

Leaning over her, he wiped her tears away. "You're just like your sister, aren't you? Gutless when it counts."

Sekorra pulled lengths of surgical tubing from his pocket and tied two strips to the headboard first. As he was attaching the other two to the footboard, his eyes kept flicking up to look at her. She tried to shift her bound hands higher, because with her buttocks resting on them, her naked pelvis was thrust upward.

He chuckled at her helpless motions. "No reason to be shy. I'm going to be seeing a lot more of you real soon."

She was running out of time. She tried to get enough oxygen to clear her brain. She needed to think quickly and clearly.

She remembered that Alec strapped a weapon to his ankle

when he jogged. What about when he slept? Did he keep a gun close? Beneath the mattress? In a bedside drawer?

No. It was no good unless she was sure. She'd have only one chance. She couldn't waste it on a weapon that might not be there.

As he'd done before, he grabbed one of her legs and tied it to the bed frame. Then he sliced though the zip tie that bound her ankles together. It didn't take just one hand to get it done. It took two. With her legs splayed apart and tied, he shoved her over onto her side. His knuckles brushed her buttocks as he sawed through the tough nylon tie that held her hands.

Swallowing her fear, she closed her eyes and tried to focus on what was happening behind her back. Timing was everything. She'd need to act fast. Surprise was her biggest weapon. Perhaps her only one.

As soon as he wrapped his fingers around one wrist, she grabbed for his crotch. She clamped down on him, at the same time throwing her upper body up off the mattress and sinking her teeth into his gut.

Cursing, he jerked back, releasing her other hand. But she hadn't hurt him enough. He immediately retaliated. He slashed at her with the knife. He didn't seem to realize that the blade wasn't fully extended, that the wounds to her arms and hands were superficial. Nor had he noticed her hand diving between the mattress and the box spring again and again.

"You're a dead woman," he yelled.

Her fingers closed over the cold, hard steel of a gun. Katie jerked it free and, bringing it up, aimed it. She had expected him to back off, but the gun seemed to fuel his fury.

"Bitch!"

She fired once. He faltered. She watched as anger

briefly disintegrated into stunned surprise. He looked at her and as he did, smiled. Even if she emptied the gun into him, would it be enough to stop him?

Already on the edge of the bed, she suddenly tumbled backward and onto the wood floor, hitting her head. The surgical tubing tightened like nooses around her ankles. The gun dropped beside her. She scooped it up, but never got the chance to aim it as a second blast propelled his body backward onto the bed.

And then Alec was there. He shoved Sekorra's limp, bleeding body aside and, scooping Katie into his arms, lifted her onto the bed. As he wrapped his arms around her, the cold steel of his gun pressed against her back. She was bleeding, she was naked, and her ankles were still tied awkwardly to the bedposts, but somehow none of that mattered. She was in his arms, she was safe. They were going to live.

She lifted her face to his, her heart catching at the sight of the grim, dangerous fury etched on his handsome features. Sekorra hadn't had a chance against this determination.

Except…another few seconds, and Alec would have been too late. Her body quivered as she thought of how close they had come to losing each other. How had he found her? How had he known where to look?

But she could ask him all those things later. Other men in uniforms were streaming into the room, and she had something far more important to say in this last private moment. Something she should have said days ago. Something she'd been saying in her heart ever since Sekorra had told her she would die tonight, praying Alec could hear her.

"Hey," she said softly.

He looked down and touched her bruised cheek with gentle fingers. "Hey," he said with a jagged breath. She realized there were tears in his eyes.

"I just wanted to say—" She tried to steady her voice, but suddenly she was shaking all over as the incoming waves of relief met the lingering aftershocks of terror. His arms tightened around her, stilling her trembling, shielding her naked body from the other men. Creating a cocoon of safety.

"I just wanted to say I love you."

Epilogue

With a grin on her face, Katie waded out into the crystal-line, seventy-two-degree water of Hidden Spring, one of the more remote springs in the State Park. Turning, she smiled up at Alec.

She'd spent the past hour in front of her easel and he had just finished his usual six-mile run though Deep Water Springs State Park, the last mile of which would have been at a hard sprint.

Using the bottom of his T-shirt, he wiped the sweat from his face. "What are you doing?"

"What does it look like I'm doing?" As she backed away, she released the top few buttons of her blouse. It was a beautiful day, one of those January ones that seemed more spring than winter. The sun hung high in a deep blue Florida sky and a gentle breeze carried the scent of the nearby vegetation and the pristine water.

It had been nearly two months since that night. Night-mares still haunted her, but when she woke up screaming, Alec's arms were always there to hold and comfort her. Most days she sensed that he had finally made peace with what had happened. Part of him would always mourn Jill's death and the death of the child she'd been carrying, but he no longer seemed consumed by it. He'd been smiling more. Katie wanted to think she was at least partly responsible.

As for her demons, the most important of them had been laid to rest with Sekorra. Somewhere deep inside Katie—a place where twins were able to communicate with one another no matter what barrier separated them— she knew Karen was finally at peace.

Katie still hadn't told her parents the whole story. Somehow, it seemed better not to. Two weeks ago, Carlos had suddenly turned up in New Orleans. Her missing paintings had yet to surface. But the paintings were strangely unimportant now. She could always paint more. And her new work was better than the old, as if she knew more about life now, as if she could finally really see that every blade of grass was beautiful, every drop of sunshine precious.

Katie bent forward, dragging the tips of her fingers through the cool water. How many days like this one had she let go by without really experiencing them? How many times had she let herself worry about things that, in the end, meant nothing?

She closed her eyes and just listened. Squirrel chatter. A blue jay's harsh complaint. The wind touching her cheek. The slow drip as water dribbled from her fingertips. She flexed her toes into the silt bottom. It was unbelievably soft, almost like standing on a cloud.

She opened her eyes, her gaze immediately searching for Alec. He no longer stood at the top of the short embankment, but at the water's edge.

She flicked water at him. "Coming in?"

"No."

"I guess I'll have to do something to change your mind about that." She pulled off the shirt and threw it at him, laughing now. She'd never felt as exposed as she did at this moment. Standing there naked from the waist up. But it was a good feeling. A freeing one.

Alec shook his head, but he was smiling. "It's January."

"And your point is?" She unfastened the front of her jeans and pushed them off her hips and down her legs, enjoying the first stirring of air against more newly exposed skin. Her pulse kicked a bit harder now. With her recklessness. With anticipation.

"You're going to get us arrested," he warned as he ripped his T-shirt over his head.

As always, something caught deep inside when he looked at her that way.

"Don't worry," she said. She finally managed to get her jeans off and threw them toward him. They fell short and dropped into the water. Covering her mouth, she laughed. "Oops."

He plucked them out and pitched them over a nearby limb. In almost the same motion, he kicked off his running shoes, and then peeled off his sweats and tossed them with her jeans.

He waded out toward her. She didn't need to lower her gaze to know how much he wanted her. It was in his eyes as he reached for her. It was in his arms as he pulled her into them. It was in his mouth as he kissed her deeply and thoroughly.

"Hey," he said when he finally lifted his lips from hers.

She was feeling a little weak in the knees. "Hey," she answered shakily.

He tilted her head back, so that the dappled sunshine could pour over it. Sunshine, she thought, as its warmth stroked her cheek. Finally sunshine instead of shadows.

"I just wanted to say—" He kissed her neck, and a trembling started deep inside her. "I just wanted to say, I love you."

* * * * *

Turn the page for a bonus look at
the next title in Lori L. Harris's
BLADE BROTHERS OF COUGAR COUNTY
miniseries: #907 SECRET ALIBI
March 2006

Chapter One

Deep Water, Florida, 10:30 p.m.

What had happened to him?

Unable to move, unable even to lift his head off the desk blotter, Dan Dawson attempted to focus on his surroundings, but couldn't. The room—his home office—seemed to be a mishmash of colors, one bleeding into another.

The objects closest to him were clearer—the paper clip and the gold pen appeared almost jewel-like as they floated against a deep red background. Those a few inches beyond were blurred and indistinct.

As he was staring at the paper clip, his eyelids slammed shut, cutting off the one sense that seemed to be working, the one thing that kept him feeling connected to his surroundings. Even as the panic ripped through him, he tried to fight it. But it was as if he'd been closed into a box—a coffin.

His eyelids suddenly sprang open, the sharp reentry of light painful, but not unbearable.

Don't panic. Panic was counterproductive.

Stay calm. Approach it as if it was one of his patients who was in trouble. He needed to…he needed to do…

What? He tried to focus, but it was as if his brain had locked him out.

Vitals. Like a life ring, the word suddenly floated past in the black sea of nothingness, and he grabbed on tight. If he really concentrated, he realized he could feel the air moving in and out of his chest. Respiration slow and shallow, but steady.

A sudden explosion of pain struck at the base of his skull, then ravaged downward through him, sucking the air from his lungs. His throat muscles contracted hard, and he felt his body gasp for oxygen.

What the hell was wrong with him?

His sluggish mind grappled with and discarded possible diagnoses. Stroke? Too young. Cardiomyopathy? Overdose? He hadn't taken any drugs in months...or had he? Had he taken something tonight?

Sweat slid slowly down his back, morphing into a living thing, a parasite that devoured his life force before escaping through his pores and oozing downward toward the floor, toward escape. Like rats from a burning building.

A distorted sound shattered the silence. Not in the room with him, but in the foyer or the kitchen. He felt a warm rush of relief. Rescue. He would be rescued. 9-1-1 would be called...

Dan again tried to raise his head, but it was like trying to lift a watermelon that dangled from the end of a swizzle stick.

When he attempted to speak, the muscles of his throat refused to cooperate, the sound coming out more a cough than a plea.

More noise drifted from beyond the room. Drawers opening. Closing. Not in a hurry, but slowly, as if someone wanted to go unheard. A shapeless shadow entered the room. For a moment, he thought he'd imagined the movement, but then, as the form passed in front of the flickering from the fireplace, he realized he hadn't.

Dan again tried to speak, but the pitifully weak sound that came from his lips was barely audible. "Help."

The shadow made no attempt to render aid. Dan's vision partially cleared, and he made out a hand encased in latex. The disembodied hand hovered ghostlike, and then slowly slid open the top right drawer of the desk.

With sudden lucidity, Dan knew what had left him paralyzed. Worse, he knew what was about to happen.

And this time, there was no controlling the panic.

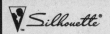

INTIMATE MOMENTS™

The MEN of MAYES COUNTY

THERE'S NOTHING LIKE A HOMETOWN HERO...

After a tornado destroys his garage, mechanic Darryl Andrew realizes that more than his livelihood needs rebuilding—his marriage to Faith Meyehauser is crumbling, too. Will the buried secrets stirred up by the storm tear apart their family...or let some fresh air into their relationship?

A HUSBAND'S WATCH

BY KAREN TEMPLETON

Silhouette Intimate Moments #1407

AVAILABLE AT YOUR FAVORITE RETAIL OUTLET.